DEATH IN VAIN

— AN EVE SAWYER MYSTERY —

DEATH IN VAIN

— AN EVE SAWYER MYSTERY —

JANE SUEN

Death in Vain: An Eve Sawyer Mystery

Jane Suen books are available for order through Ingram Press Catalogues.

www.janesuen.com

Printed in the United States of America

First Printing: November 2025

Ebook ISBN: 978-1-951002-36-7

Paperback ISBN: 978-1-951002-37-4

Audiobook ISBN: 978-1-951002-38-1

In loving memory of my father

AUTHOR'S NOTE

Inspired by small towns in the rural South that are tiny dots on the map, flyspecks of a town, this book is a work of fiction.

P.S. For those wondering, like I was after writing this book, how small a town can be and still be a town... check out the incorporated town of Monowi, Nebraska, with a population of one.

PROLOGUE

She lay there on the hard asphalt, her limbs splayed out on the rough surface of the aging two-lane highway. The long tresses of her thick dark hair were entangled with bits of dirt, decayed leaves, and pine needles.

The heat of the day was long gone. The bright sunlight retreated as the darkness of the night emerged. An hour later, the moonlight, unobscured by clouds, cast shadows over this lonely stretch of rural road.

The whisper of wind in the trees made a soft rustling, joining with the harmonious chirping of crickets and other sounds of nature.

A normal summer night.

Except for the woman on the road.

Her lifeless eyes open, seeing nothing.

CHAPTER ONE

It was near the end of summer. I packed light for my getaway before school started—essential toiletries and a few changes of clothing. I told no one except my mom. She understood why.

The murder case in Prospect had drained my energy and left me with barely any reserves. It turned out to be more than I had bargained for when I agreed to help my friend Bob. I couldn't say "no" to my friends. Not then and not ever. But it was impossible to see at the beginning how much effort it would take to uncover the dark secrets and expose the killers. It had sapped me, taking my strength and depleting my vigor. Both my body and soul needed to be recharged, and I had precious time left in the last carefree days of summer before the start of another hectic school year. I took charge of my welfare and escaped, to go miles away by myself, where I could relax in peace and quiet. No work. No distractions.

I took my cell phone because I promised my mom she'd have a way to reach me. She asked me where I was going. I couldn't say.

It was the truth. I didn't make plans and had no destination in mind.

I got in my ratty old car and drove out of town, heading north to the highway.

For the first hundred miles or so, I was still feeling high, soaring free of responsibilities and schedules. I had no commitments, no place where I had to be. I kept my foot on the pedal, sometimes a little too heavy, as I maneuvered the curves and climbs and descents, speeding ahead with the goal to put as many miles behind me as possible. The day was bright, and the sky was crisp blue, with the sun beating down mercilessly. I had left my sunglasses behind at home, but nothing could dampen my spirits.

CHAPTER TWO

ANOTHER COUPLE OF HOURS LATER, MY EXUBERANCE deflated to monotony after endless stretches of asphalt and the drab sameness that repeated itself mile after mile. I took an exit and got off the highway, opting for a more scenic drive on country roads that meandered across rolling hills and patches of farmland with houses and barns and fences, cows and horses, and the occasional farm equipment in a field. I eased my grip on the wheel, smiling at the sight of three horses grazing in a fenced pasture. They seemed content, carefree, just minding their own business.

Soon I would be relaxing somewhere with not a worry in the world, just like them. My smile widened with this thought. In my rush to pack and get going, I had skipped breakfast. My stomach grumbled as a reminder. This far from the highway, fast-food signs were nonexistent; nowhere to be seen were those usual food-and-fuel establishments clustered around cookie-cutter exits. A quick glance all around and in my rearview mirror showed no other vehicles in sight. I took a risk, pressing my foot on the pedal, accelerating as I pictured myself sitting down at a diner that served delicious home-cooked Southern food.

I craved a hearty meal cooked by a chef in the greasy kitchen of an establishment that didn't have yellow letters in its sign. A country restaurant owned and operated by locals, where locals eat. I watched the needle climb on the speedometer. I was hungry.

A sign appeared ahead—Dave's Place. I caught sight of a small framed house about the same time and braked hard, yanking a sharp right turn directly into the crowded parking lot.

I barely missed the vehicle ahead, which was parked facing the front door. My heartbeat raced at the close call, seeing the "Sheriff" conspicuously emblazoned on the side of the car. I guessed they were inside eating. The lot was packed. I was lucky to find a spot.

The brisk wind whipped my loose hair as I parked and got out. I gripped the car door, bracing myself, turning my face up. The sky had darkened as the sun hid behind massive gray clouds. The rumble of distant thunder gave warning of impending rain. A quick summer storm that would break the spell of a sultry afternoon and drench the earth.

I wasted no time turning on my heels toward the restaurant. A blast of air-conditioning greeted me as I stepped inside. The room was crowded and noisy and filled with loud laughter. Just my kind of greasy joint.

The hostess came by to greet me after a brief wait. "For one?" She inclined her head and smiled.

"Yes, please."

She picked up a menu and a set of utensils wrapped in a paper napkin and led the way, skirting between occupied tables and chairs pulled out in haphazard directions. I scanned the jam-packed room, looking for a seat. Every table was occupied.

The hostess made her way toward the only empty seat, the last stool at the end of the counter. "How about there?"

To its left sat two uniformed officers, their backs to me. No doubt it was their cruiser in the parking lot. My heartbeat quickened with a rush of guilt about my speeding. I looked down at the stool, the seat painted bright red.

"Is this okay?" the hostess asked, uncertain.

"Yes, it's fine, thank you." I was grateful she had found me a seat. I should be so lucky, right?

She nodded and quickly placed the menu and utensils on the counter as I sat, then she hurried away.

This trip was to get away from crime and murder, and yet there they were—two law enforcement officers sitting right next to me.

The waitress working behind the counter appeared, wiping some water rings away. "Something to drink?" she asked.

I looked at her. A young girl, long hair tied back in a

ponytail, tendrils escaping around her pretty face. It was devoid of makeup, except for a flush on her cheeks, which could have been because of the heat of the kitchen or the nature of her job. She wore a maroon T-shirt with the name of the diner, Dave's Place, printed on the front, and dark jeans. A short black apron with pockets crammed, an order pad sticking out of one, was tied over her T-shirt, encircling her trim waist.

"Coffee," I said without hesitation.

"Sugar and cream?" Her voice was bright and chirpy despite the tired look in her eyes.

"Black, please."

"What are you having, hon?" She waited with pen in hand, poised over her order pad.

A typed slip of paper with today's special of burgers and fries was clipped to the frayed menu. Not finding any veggie burgers, I scanned the menu for the side orders of vegetables. "I'll take green beans, mac and cheese, mashed potatoes, and fried okra, please," I said, relying on familiar Southern fare. Couldn't go wrong with that.

"Them's my favorites," the waitress drawled in a voice laced with a Southern accent as she moved away to place my order.

I didn't have to wait long for the coffee. She winked as she set my mug down before turning to the two officers with an almost full coffee carafe.

"Care for a fill-up, hon?"

I detected a slight familiarity in her voice and a

gaze that was a fraction of a second longer on the younger of the two men. But maybe she called everyone "hon."

The older man spoke up. "We'll take them to go, Caitlin."

My eyes swung to her name tag, partially hidden behind a wisp of her long tawny hair.

She came back to them quickly with two large to-go-cups. "Y'all get any shut-eye last night?"

The older man shook his head and sighed as he picked up their tabs and headed toward the cashier by the front door. The younger man reached out to grab the coffees, his fingers grazing Caitlin's.

Caitlin blushed as she cleared their dishes. She came back and wiped the counter again, glancing at me. "You want a refill?"

"Sure, thanks. No hurry, just when you have time."

She came back with my food and filled my mug from a half-full pot of coffee.

"Thanks, Caitin," I said, smiling. "I'm Eve, by the way."

I was curious about her exchange with the sheriff's deputies. I tipped my head toward their empty chairs. "Long night, huh?"

She sighed. "They've been at it for hours."

"At *it*?"

"Yeah, they were called to the scene of a crime."

"What happened?" The words popped out of my mouth before I could think.

She leaned in, lowering her voice. "A dead body."

She shifted the pot to her other hand. "The first we've had since I can remember."

"Were you born here?"

"Yup, been here all my life." She looked young to me, about my age or younger. "Nineteen years," she said, as if she'd read my mind.

"What's the name of this town?" I hadn't noticed a sign driving in.

"Vain," she said, quickly adding, "but it's a flyspeck of a town. We don't even have our own police force. The county sheriff's office in Bearsville covers our area."

"You know what happened?"

"Somebody found a body on the road. Called it in to nine-one-one."

I took a deep breath. What were the chances there'd be a body on my getaway? I was passing through. But despite myself, I couldn't help asking more questions. "Do they know the identity of the person who died?"

Caitlin paused. Her eyes had a faraway look.

"Was it someone you knew?"

"Kaylee," she said softly.

"Small place, everyone knows everyone?"

"Yeah, that's the way it is here. We went to school together. But not in the same class. She was a year younger than me."

"I'm sorry." I could see she was visibly moved and affected.

She shook her head and licked her lips, apparently needing to talk, or perhaps she was an incurable gossip even to a stranger. "I probably shouldn't say this, but I've heard some things." Her eyes flicked to the empty stools next to me.

The way she'd acted with the younger deputy, it was subtle but there. Maybe it was partly shyness, although I thought there was a hint of familiarity. Perhaps he had let slip something when they talked. A detail about the dead girl. Perhaps he had never seen a dead person in the line of duty, or perhaps it had been a gruesome, violent death and he couldn't deal with it yet, and so he spoke out of turn.

Caitlin picked up the rag and wiped the counter yet again, rubbing the same area over and over. "We were all in a state of shock when we heard. She was the girl everyone thought would go far. You know, everybody thought she'd make it out of here. Go places. Do things. Maybe become rich and famous."

"I'm sorry for your loss." I struggled to find the words. "Did she have a family?"

"Yeah, her mom and an older sis."

"No father?"

"He left when she was a baby and her parents divorced."

"Do they know what happened?"

"No ... I don't know." Caitlin's slight frame sagged and her perky stance deflated, as if the weight of it all sat on her shoulders.

I pondered the information. Time was critical. "The sheriff's department is working hard on this, right?"

She sighed. "Yeah, they're trying. Don't know how long they can last without sleep."

"Caitlin, next order is ready," a guy shouted from the kitchen.

She sighed again and turned to go, her waitress smile back on. But it didn't quite reach her eyes.

CHAPTER THREE

The parking lot had mostly cleared by the time I finished eating and went outside, signaling the end of the lunch period. I took my time, walking on the wet surface to my car and stepping carefully over the slick areas. The sky was blue again after the burst of showers, and the sun was back out.

I hesitated when I reached my car, key in hand. *Do I stay in this town, or keep driving?* I was torn.

I had no place I had to be, and nothing on my schedule until the start of classes next week. No one was waiting for me at the other end of my trip. I was totally free to do whatever I wanted to do and go as far as I wanted to go.

I didn't know these people. I was a stranger in town. Just someone passing by. Nobody knew me. Nobody had asked me to help. But my mind wandered back to what Caitlin had said and how shook up she was. The worry on her face. The overworked deputies. Kaylee. Could I just go, knowing what I'd leave behind?

I unlocked my car, got in, sat down, and put the key in the ignition. I leaned back and closed my eyes. The dead girl. No explanation. I let my mind wander. They had an investigation going, and two deputies were already working the case.

But I couldn't just drive out of town. Not just yet, when I didn't have to go.

I sat up straight, having arrived at a decision. A temporary one. It felt right. It *was* right. I breathed out slowly, letting go of the tension in my struggle.

Across the street from the diner, the Pines Motel had a flashing red "Vacancy" sign. The building was a flat, one-story cinder-block structure. Its pale green paint looked like it had weathered many seasons. The place had clearly seen its better days. But the grass was cut, and the bushes were trimmed in the front. Remnants of crushed flowers hinted at a fuller flower bed at one time. In terms of my expenses, I figured it would be cheap accommodations going by the cost of the meal I just had.

I decided to stay a day or two, then I'd reassess my options. First, I needed to check in and get a room. I drove the short distance across the street and parked.

The motel clerk was young, a teenager. Probably still in high school or already working right out of school. He eyed me with interest when I walked in. "Help you?"

"Hi, I'd like a room, please." I was glad he didn't call me "ma'am." I was close to his age.

"We're full," he said.

I looked around the empty lobby. This place didn't seem to be hopping and bopping. "But you have a lit 'Vacancy' sign."

He shrugged as if it was an insignificant detail.

"Could you double-check, please? I ... I really need a room tonight."

He looked at his computer screen and clicked a few times with the mouse.

I gulped. "Is ... is it full?"

He didn't respond. He still had his face in front of the screen as his fingers scrolled. "Hmm..."

I watched him as he checked. Either way, I kept quiet. He'd tell me when he was ready.

A more clicks, this time a staccato beat to it, a bit more frantic. Then he picked up the phone and dialed. Someone apparently answered, and he whispered into the mouthpiece. I heard him ask about a room, but I didn't catch the number.

"Is the room occupied?" he asked. I could hear someone talking on the other end, but I couldn't make out the words. Then a pause. "Didn't check out ... It's in the system ... No, not paid," he said. A longer pause. "What? ... A 'Do Not Disturb' sign is hanging on the doorknob?" He raised his voice as if irritated. "I *know* we're not supposed to ... Please go check," he said, drumming his fingers on the counter.

I drew in a breath. He glared at me and held up a finger on his lips to keep silent.

Another pause, and then he spoke firmly and quickly. "I've got someone here now who wants to rent a room. Put it in storage. Okay, let me know." He hung up the phone abruptly.

"You don't have a reservation?" he asked me.

I assumed it was a rhetorical question. "No, I'm passing through."

"Can you come back in about thirty minutes?"

I had heard enough to feel hopeful after piecing together his one-sided conversation. "I'll be back. Thanks." I gave him a smile as I walked out.

CHAPTER FOUR

I LEFT THE CAR PARKED IN FRONT OF THE MOTEL AND took off for a walk. I got on the road, heading north, passing Dave's Place.

Soon the days would be cooler and the leaves would turn fall colors. Now was the perfect time to enjoy the last lazy days at the end of summer before heading back to campus and the flurry of back-to-school activities.

The pine forest provided shade and a serene environment, far from the rest of the world. I felt a gentle breeze on my cheeks. Ahead, the ground sloped around the curve. Looking back, I could see the roadside restaurant. Across from it, the motel sign pointed to the building in the back, at the end of a gravel road. It was secluded, nestled under the lofty trees, surrounded by a carpet of leaves, scattered pine cones, and needles on the ground below.

I breathed in deeply, taking in a lungful of fresh

pine-scented air. It was quiet and beautiful. I'd stumbled upon a piece of heaven here. If I hadn't stopped at the diner, I would've missed the motel. If I'd missed the diner, I wouldn't have known about the body. This getaway trip was to *get away* from death and murder. To get a reprieve before diving back into another busy fall semester. Not to see, think, or have anything to do with unsolved crimes. But as much as I didn't seek them, and even as I left home and sought a peaceful trip and time to regroup, how far behind was death? Not far, in this case. It was ahead on this road.

I shook my head to clear my thoughts. I shivered at the pull of something that brought me here, in this direction, on this road. Checking the time, I saw I had a few minutes to spare to run back to the motel. If they had a place for me, I was going to take it. I couldn't pass it by. I had to stay. Maybe it was fate that brought me here. I turned around and headed back.

CHAPTER FIVE

Back at the Pines Motel office, I noticed the "Vacancy" sign was now unlit. I went in.

The same guy was at the desk. This time, his name tag, which read "MC," was pinned to his shirt.

I waved. "I'm back."

He didn't go to any length to explain what happened. MC got on the computer, typed a few keystrokes, and nodded. "I need your credit card," he said before I had a chance to ask.

My heartbeat quickened. I fumbled with my purse and retrieved it, handing it to him. "You mean …"

MC ignored me, focusing on my credit card before proceeding to run it through, pausing to ask, "How many nights will you be staying?"

"Uh, two nights, please," I blurted out. "Although I may stay longer. Would I be able to add more dates later?"

"You need to let me know the day before, by eleven." He held my gaze.

I nodded, taking my card back. "By the way, what happened to the last guest?"

"We took care of it." He whipped out the key and shoved it in my hand to signal our transaction was done. "Room 6."

"Thank you." I didn't pry further. Nor did I look back as I walked out the door.

The rooms were numbered in sequence straight down, with brass numbers tacked on each door. My unit was the last one.

It was a nondescript, basic room. The drapes on the window were partially open, letting in daylight across the worn, faded carpet. In front of it, there was a small round table and a chair. A double bed was present, and it had a frayed cover. Next to it was a nightstand with a lamp, alarm clock, and telephone. A chest of drawers and a medium-sized TV rounded out the furniture. There was a microwave, no fridge. No coffee maker. The walls were bare except for a cheap framed print of a bird hanging opposite the bed.

The bathroom was barely big enough to fit a tiny sink, toilet, and shower. A folded bath towel that was once white, but now dulled from countless washes, hung on the towel rack. The shelf above the toilet held two more neatly folded towels.

The room was at least clean. All the basics were present, with no fancy stuff. It was simple, but it would suffice.

I quickly unpacked my few belongings. I took my shoes off and stretched out on the bed, fluffing the double-stacked pillows under my head until I was comfortable.

I dozed off. I didn't know how long. I woke up groggily, my eyes blurry and unfocused. For a moment, I panicked, finding myself in an unfamiliar room. Then it came to me, the bird's beady dark eyes staring at me from across the bed. I picked up the TV remote and clicked it on. Loud music blasted away. Fluttering flags flashed on the screen and big, bright orange banners with "Al's Used Cars" and "Gigantic Sale on NOW" grabbed for my attention. I dropped the remote on the bed and watched a brassy used-car salesman, presumably Al himself, talking and gesturing to his stable of cars in the lot. He wore a purple suit with a red tie and smoked a cigar. He talked a mile a minute and sang and danced his way around the lot, stopping to point out enticing specials on cars that were washed and waxed and buffed so much that they shined and sparkled. The finale was a line of potential buyers, all singing and dancing, snaking their way around the lot with Al at the head, then stopping at the gigantic sale sign. The ad was so corny, I had to smile. I couldn't help humming the tune.

I thought of my ratty old car. Trustworthy. Familiar. Mine. I had bought it secondhand, or thirdhand. Actually, I didn't know how many hands it had passed through. The previous owner had put an ad in the school paper. When I called the number, she was eager to sell. I had asked her why. As it turned out, she was a student and about to graduate. She was unloading her car and other stuff to move to Europe. "Interested?" She'd asked, going further to list the upgrades to the car, including a new set of tires and brake pads. I went to see the vehicle. Took a test drive. Asked a mechanic friend of a friend to check it out. I had fallen in love with the car when I saw it, nicks and dents and all, but I waited until he checked out. Hefty car repairs weren't in my budget. It was a keeper. No, I would not trade it in. I chuckled ... Al could keep his cars.

Different music blared, accompanied by a TV station banner, heralding the five p.m. local news from Channel 5 in Bearsville. I quickly searched the map on my cell phone and found it twenty-eight miles away. A news conference popped on the screen. It was airing live. Standing in front of the mic and speaking in an authoritative voice was a hefty, ruddy-looking man in a perfectly pressed khaki uniform. He introduced himself as Sheriff Waco. Off to the side, I recognized the two deputies who had been sitting next to me at the diner. They stood in the back with hands clasped, looking somber and serious, alongside a few other people.

I turned up the volume to hear Waco saying, "...the body of a young female was found early this morning on the road..." His voice caught as he struggled to speak. I heard the words "possible hit-and-run" and "fatality" as he continued, the sentences broken up as I strove to listen.

My eyes fixed on the TV screen, stunned, unable to turn away as a close-up of a map appeared with a red dot to note the location. "Victim's identity has been confirmed," the sheriff said. Then a photo flashed with the name "Kaylee Davenport." A beautiful heart-shaped face, smiling, lips slightly parted. Gorgeous long hair loosely styled.

They played a clip from an earlier video, showing barrier stands, red cones, and yellow crime-scene tape on the road where the body had been found. Sheriff's department cars had blocked the area on both sides, and deputies were directing traffic around the scene where parked vehicles and first responders had gathered.

As the news conference wrapped up, the parting shot showed a bit of the road in the distance and the last of the sheriff's cars leaving.

Sheriff Waco looked like he got little sleep. Lips pinched and eyes sunken with a weariness that went beyond tiredness. He gave out the sheriff's office phone number, then looked directly at the camera and said, "If you saw or heard anything—*anything* at all—please call us immediately."

CHAPTER SIX

I SPENT THE NIGHT TOSSING AND TURNING, UNABLE TO get a good sleep. I woke up early the next morning to bright sunlight. It all came back to me as I looked around my motel room. Where I was. What I was doing here.

I suddenly felt a powerful urge to leave this drab place and run outside, to feel the warmth of the sun on my face and bare arms. Hear the chirping of birds in the morning hours. See the sky, pine trees, and forest bathed in the sun's glow. Smell fresh air. To escape the darkness and horrors that hounded me at night.

I dressed quickly and walked out.

The gravel crunched under my shoes as I slammed the motel door, ignoring the rough edges pressing against my shoes. It was time to get new ones, but I couldn't bear to toss them yet. I rested my hand on the car door and took a deep breath, again filling my lungs with clean air. I got in my car and started it, easing out onto the road.

I drove slowly, glancing in my rearview mirror at the receding restaurant and the motel and checking the miles on the odometer to mark the distance. It was as if something propelled me to go this way even though a part of me wanted to run as far away from the scene as possible. I kept going, impatient at the wait and yet forestalling the inevitable. I knew the police had already processed the scene and taken pictures and evidence. The body would be gone, of course. The space would be cleared. I knew it wasn't too far, perhaps a mile or two.

I inched on, alert for oncoming traffic and keeping an eye out on the road, half expecting to see a crowd or yellow tape, half wondering how I would find the spot if they removed the crime tape, barriers, and cones.

I caught movement ahead, a flutter of red. I slowed down, pulled off the highway, and rolled to a stop before the spot, which was a couple of feet off to the side of the road, and got out of the car.

A ruffled scarf was tied to a wooden cross. I walked toward the makeshift memorial. Already there were flower bouquets wrapped in clear plastic, with a smattering of notes and cards tucked among them. Two pieces of rough wood were used to make the cross; someone painted them white with uneven brushstrokes and hung red ribbons and a wreath on it. Propped in front of the cross was a framed photograph of Kaylee. The same photo from the news conference.

I knelt on the patch of flattened ground at eye level. The tumble of thick long curls framed her face, the skin smooth and unblemished. Eyes bright and full of youthful simplicity and vitality. Lips lifted in a smile, showing straight teeth. Trusting, innocent, full of promise. At the cusp of adulthood.

Now her life was gone. Her eyes would never see the light of day again, their sparkle forever dulled, only to shrivel and sink in the sockets. I swallowed, choking back the urge to cry.

"A shame, ain't it?"

I stiffened at the sound of the masculine voice, startled by the ill-timed and unwelcome intrusion. I turned, standing up as a shadow cast over me and a hand came into view, gripping a single long-stemmed red rose. The man placed it gently on the ground by Kaylee's photo.

"A crying shame." His voice softened, breaking into a raspy whisper. A mournful look was on his craggy, unshaven face. He stood there with his arms slack and his hands empty. His long-limbed body sagged, as if he lacked the strength to hold himself upright.

I grabbed his arm to steady him. It was sinewy under the thin cotton of his rolled-down shirtsleeves. I felt his muscles. Despite his thinness, he was not frail. Yet his eyes betrayed him in this weak moment.

He shrugged my hand off, looking at me with an embarrassed expression, as if he realized he had let his guard down in front of a stranger.

"Are you...?" I asked.

"I'm Lance," he said. "And you are?"

"Eve."

"I don't believe we've met. You're new here?"

"Just got into town."

"A friend of Kaylee's?" he asked.

"No, I didn't know her."

He threw me a quizzical look. "Then who are you?"

"Let's start over. My name is Eve Sawyer. I'm a student at Midway College, but I'm taking some time off at the end of summer before heading back to school again. This will probably sound weird, but I needed a break because I was exhausted after helping my friend look into his uncle's death."

Lance raked his fingers through his full head of gray-streaked hair, looking more confused. "You're some kind of cop?"

"No, but I've gotten involved in a few murder cases, you know, looking for clues."

"You good at this?" Lance was direct. He kept his gaze on me, waiting for my answer. I sensed his questioning was more than casual conversion and he had something in mind.

"You could say that."

He pondered this. "So how did you get here?"

"I left on this road trip yesterday and was passing by when I got hungry," I said, pointing in the direction of the restaurant. "I had driven for hours, drinking coffee to keep alert. I finally stopped to eat when I saw Dave's Place, which was exactly what I wanted, a country diner serving home-cooked

Southern meals. And I heard about this tragedy there."

I glanced at the faint outline of chalk markings on the road, where Kaylee's body had been. It was partially on the road, but mostly over to the side across the line. My mind whirled with a rush of wild guesses and questions: How did the body end up here? Was it a hit-and-run accident? Someone driving at high speeds on a rural road? Was the body hit, rolled over? Or something else happened? Who called it in and reported it?

I turned back and saw the slight tremble of his chin. The aged look etched on his face. His stooped body. A man in grief. I knew the signs well. Lance's appearance, speech, and movements showed it. I didn't have to ask him. I didn't have to ask myself either. I knew what he was going through, but I needed more information first if I was going to stay longer and look into this tragic death.

I wanted to know where he had come from. I didn't even know his last name. Was he related to Kaylee? He hadn't introduced himself as a father. Maybe he was an uncle. I scrutinized his lined face, estimating his age. Certainly not her brother.

"Why are you asking, Lance?" I hesitated. "Er, I didn't catch your last name."

"Spencer," he said. "Lance Spencer."

"Any relation to Kaylee?"

"Uh, no," he said, stumbling.

"You're just a concerned citizen?"

His cheek muscle twitched. I detected a faint blush. Maybe he was something else, or something more.

"I ain't related by blood."

"But are you related in another way?"

"You might could say that." Lance glanced down, not meeting my eyes. "I'm her mom's *ex*-fiancé."

CHAPTER SEVEN

I took notice of the way Lance emphasized the "ex," almost spitting it out. He punctuated it with high-pitched laughter. There was no love lost there. I'd touched a raw nerve—and cracked a bit of his bravado.

"And Kaylee?"

He pulled in a deep breath. "When I met Kaylee, she was a toddler. Her daddy had left when she was a baby. Didn't want nothin' to do with either of them, the baby or her mama, Mary Belle." He paused, shaking his head. "Something inside her changed. She was bitter, all right, and she toughened up. You have to understand how it was—a single mom with an older kid, and then came a baby, another mouth to feed. She was struggling, working odd jobs here and there to make ends meet. But with a baby and all, it was even harder. If a job came up during the daytime when the older daughter was in school, she had to find a babysitter for Kaylee, and when she was lucky to find one, the little money she earned went to pay for the sitter and food. A job in the evening cost her more to pay for a sitter for two. Most times, Mary Belle was behind on her bills. But she made sure, with what little she had, that the kids didn't go hungry."

"Any help from Kaylee's father?"

Lance grunted. "Not a cent. He was a drifter. Moved so much, she lost touch. She couldn't afford an attorney to find him, go after him and make him pay. She finally gave up."

His eyes narrowed into cold, hard glints.

"How did you come into the picture?" I asked gently.

"She had car troubles, but she had no money to fix them. Mary Belle was desperate. Needed a car to get to work. She was asking everybody, and that's how she heard I was pretty handy and knew my way around car engines."

"Are you a mechanic?"

"No, but my daddy was. I'd watch him when I was little. When I got older, he'd let me help him. He taught me a lot." Lance belted out a hearty laugh. "I know my way under a hood."

"So you fixed her car, and that's how you met?"

"Not exactly. She came to me, talked to me first. Then she came out with a proposition. Bartered with me."

"To fix one thing?"

"No." Lance shook his head and grinned. "Mary Belle was shrewd. I'll give her that. She knew her car needed more than one fix. She showed me a list of several things she needed done. And it wasn't just an oil change and maintenance."

"What did she offer you?" I asked. A desperate woman like her had few options. My imagination grew colorful, but I kept it to myself.

"She was businesslike. Said we'd have lunch, a home-cooked meal, and discuss the terms of our barter." He threw back his head and laughed. "Right from the start, she got me interested."

"Was she attractive?"

He nodded.

"And?"

"And smart. She was a looker. Sexy, with curves in the right places, and a bit of extra padding in some areas."

"So you left with a barter agreement after lunch?"

His face flushed. Bright, flaming red. "We ... we didn't finish lunch," he sputtered.

CHAPTER EIGHT

Lance continued after recovering from his moment of awkward embarrassment, and related sappy stories of little Kaylee growing up. His part in helping to raise her became evident. His voice swelled with pride like a father would, having her as a daughter since she was a toddler, for about eight years, longer than any man who came after him, after he and Mary Belle broke up.

I turned away from Lance, my eyes lighting on the makeshift memorial, with the flowers and notes tucked among them. I bent down to read one. It was on a piece of torn white paper and written in pencil. The message was short. "I will miss you like no other."

Lance looked over my shoulder to read it.

"Who wrote this?" I asked.

He shrugged, shaking his head.

I pointed to a card, signed "Sis," and threw a questioning glance.

"Kaylee's older sister, Sadie."

My curiosity turned to the other cards. I picked up another one tucked inside a plain white envelope. It was a sympathy card, with a bouquet of flowers on the front, and a couple lines of condolence printed inside the card. A name was scrawled at the bottom. It was simply signed "Luke." Nothing else.

I held up the card for Lance to see.

He nodded. "Luke Adams. A high school friend. He was her boyfriend. Last I heard, they broke up."

I guess Luke was a man of few words, but he had been thoughtful enough to get a card and bring it here. I made a mental note to talk to this guy. Maybe he could shed some light on their breakup.

The shock and grief of losing Kaylee so violently were etched on Lance's face. Who would have thought this would take place in this peaceful, tiny Southern flyspeck of a place? After what I'd seen of death and murder, maybe it didn't surprise me.

I returned my gaze to the memorial. The little wooden cross bravely faced the road alone. I had seen other crosses erected by roads—sometimes at dangerous curves, blind sights, railroad crossings, roads that didn't have warning signs, places where a death took place. I had driven past these silent memorials, the only testament to the site of tragic accidents and the loss of life.

Some had survived the elements better than others. Over time, some crosses were leaning over, weakened and weathered. Some had aged, become dilapidated, with faded paint and rotting wood. Some were bare, the flowers long lost, scattered by the wind across fields and hills. I felt sadness at the lives lost. I often wondered what had happened as I drove by. But I had kept going. I never knew the answer.

Maybe it was time I stopped to find out.

This time.

Maybe fate destined me to travel here.

This place.

Here and now.

CHAPTER NINE

I started by asking Lance questions and getting Mary Belle's and Luke's contact information. He gave me their phone numbers and addresses and told me to call if I had questions.

"Is Sadie living at home with Mary Belle?"

"Yes, she is. Kaylee was too."

"What was Kaylee's relationship with her mother?"

"I don't know how to describe it," Lance said. "Their relationship was up and down. When Kaylee was a child, she was as sweet as can be. But she developed a rebellious streak in her teens. She became demanding, emboldened. Picked fights with her mother. They've had screaming matches. Mary Belle couldn't handle her then."

"Were you still in the picture?"

"Naw, we had split long before that. But I helped out every so often."

"Fixing cars?"

"Yeah, cars, things around the house, stuff that broke. I'm pretty handy." He hesitated, then said, "Mary Belle also asked me to help with Kaylee. Said she was at her wit's end."

"You got along with Kaylee?"

He smiled. "She was a bright child. When her mother was working, she used to tag along with me. I'd take her on minor jobs. If I wasn't working, I'd take her fishing."

"Fishing?"

"She had a knack for it." His face lit up, and he flashed a grin. "I bought her a child's rain suit. She was the cutest little fisherman, dressed in a rain jacket and pants with a hat and rubber rain boots. But when she got older—" His voice cracked. He struggled, holding back his emotions.

"When she got older?" I prodded.

"She changed."

"Did you still go fishing?"

He shook his head slowly. "She had outgrown her little rain suit. And we didn't go out fishing no more."

"You were still engaged to her mother?"

"We were going through some shaky ground. It was rocky between her mother and me. Mary Belle and I called it quits soon after."

"Did you see Kaylee much after the breakup with her mother?"

"Her mother asked me to help when Kaylee got out of hand. It had gotten so bad, Mary Belle couldn't deal with it. She didn't know that Kaylee had come to me even before that. Confided in me. I promised Kaylee I'd keep her confidence. I didn't tell Kaylee, either, what her mother had asked me to do."

I chewed on this. He was talking to both women. They trusted him. They didn't know the other had confided in him.

"Did you have anything to do with Kaylee's death?" I said gently, asking the obligatory question.

"No!" he spat, throwing me a look that said it all. His lips pursed with anger, like a man unjustly insulted. I knew better than to assume anything, even the obvious. Sometimes especially the obvious. But at the end of the day, I always had to ask.

"Know anyone who'd want to hurt Kaylee?"

He shook his head again, answering without hesitation. "No, not like this. She wasn't a saint, but she didn't deserve *this*." He sighed.

CHAPTER TEN

On the way to Mary Belle's place, the picture Lance had painted of Kaylee, a sweet child turned troubled teenager, stuck in my mind. And of Mary Belle, a single mother working constantly to make ends meet, who couldn't handle her rebellious child. Both women confided in him after he was no longer their boyfriend/fiancé and stepdad-to-be.

I didn't have far to go to find Mary Belle's house. It was a modest wooden structure painted white. A skimpy porch bordered by thin railings ran across the front. The place had an air of simplicity and economy. No room for frills or extravagance. The house was kept neat and the lawn tidy.

I parked, walked up the steps, and stood on the porch, scanning the windows for a sign of anyone home, but the blinds were drawn and I couldn't see inside. I paused at the door and listened for a sound before I knocked, giving a couple of rapid taps. Waited, then knocked again. Still no sound. "Hello, anybody home?"

I heard the distinct squeak of a screen door opening, then a woman's voice hollered, "She ain't home."

I turned toward the sound and saw a heavyset woman standing on the porch of the house next door. "When will she be back?"

"Who wants to know?" she bellowed as I walked down the steps and crossed the tiny yard toward her.

"I'm Eve Sawyer."

She scrutinized my face, as if reaching deep in her memory banks, then shook her head like she had come up with nothing. "I ain't seen you around before."

"No, ma'am," I said. "Lance gave me this address for Mary Belle."

The woman's round, youthful face lit up. "You're a friend of Lance's."

"I just met him." I gave her a recap of our meeting at the makeshift memorial and the reason I was here. I said, "I'm sorry to hear about Kaylee," when I finished.

At the mention of Kaylee, her demeanor changed. Her face softened and her mouth trembled. "It's a shame what happened to that girl," she mumbled.

"Can we talk?" I clutched the strap of my purse. I sensed she had a kind heart beneath her blustery, crusty exterior. Maybe she could tell me more. Every neighborhood had an inquisitive neighbor, and she could be one of those who knew everybody's business.

She pushed her door wide open. "C'mon in."

The aroma of cinnamon greeted me as I stepped in.

It brought back a rush of warm, nostalgic feelings from my childhood. Of coming home after school. Somehow my mother timed my arrival with fresh-baked cinnamon buns hot out of the oven. It was a once-a-week treat I looked forward to, and an implicit reward for doing my homework after school and being an excellent student.

I couldn't wipe the silly smile off my face. The woman noticed and grinned. "I made cinnamon buns. Brewed a fresh pot of coffee. Would you like some?"

"Yes, ma'am," I said, nodding with enthusiasm.

"You can call me Betty Lou." She gestured to the sofa. "Have a seat."

I sat on the soft, comfy sofa and glanced around the room. A cushioned chair, some magazines tossed on the coffee table, books and knickknacks stuffed on the bookshelves, framed pictures hung on the wall. It exuded a warm, well-lived-in vibe.

Betty Lou appeared with a plate of cinnamon buns, placing them on the coffee table, and went back to the kitchen and came back with two mugs of steaming coffee and a fistful of napkins. "Help yourself," she said as she sat down on the sofa.

I reached for a warm bun and sank my teeth into the gooey, sweet icing and soft dough. "Mm-mm," I mumbled, chewing with my eyes closed, enjoying every bit. It was so good. I sucked the icing from my sticky fingers and helped myself to the pile of napkins. "My mom used to make these," I said. "Your buns are delicious."

She responded with a wide grin. "Why, thank you, dear. It was my daughter's favorite. She begged me to make them all the time."

I glanced around the room as if looking for her.

"Danielle's gone now. Moved to the city." Betty Lou made a motion, waving her hand.

"Does she come home often?"

"Not as often as I'd like." She heaved a sigh.

I took a swig of coffee and set my mug on the table. "You're a friend of Lance's?"

"Yeah. It's more like the other way around. He's been a good friend to me. One time, he noticed my grass was gettin' high and needin' cutting, and he just went and did it. He did other things, too, to help me. But he didn't ask for money. Just did it."

"Was this when he lived with Mary Belle?"

"Yeah, at first. Then later, after they broke up, he'd come back every so often and he'd do something for me." She nodded her head. "I'd make sure I had baked goodies for him."

"What was his favorite?"

She laughed, throwing her chin up. "Cinnamon buns."

We talked more, mostly about Lance. It was clear Betty Lou adored him and considered any friend of Lance's a friend of hers. After about five minutes, I steered the conversation back to why I was here.

"I'm sorry about Kaylee."

"The poor girl." Her voice broke. "It ... it was a shock to all of us."

"How's Mary Belle?" I asked. "Is she here?"

"She's holed up in the house. Totally drained dry after the police left. She needed to lie down and rest." Betty Lou looked me straight in the eye and gave me a stern look. "You'd best leave her alone for now."

I nodded. Message delivered. The last thing I wanted was to be rude and intrude on a grieving and exhausted mother.

"Where's Sadie?"

"She left earlier."

"Any idea where she went?"

"Seemed in a hurry," Betty Lou mumbled. "The way things were with her mother…"

I frowned. "With her mother?"

Betty Lou drew a deep breath. "Kaylee was her mother's favorite. Mary Belle made no secret of that. It was Kaylee this and Kaylee that—she was always talking about Kaylee. Her beautiful daughter, who would be a famous model or actress one day. She felt elated after Kaylee was born. Mary Belle focused her attention and all her hopes and dreams on pretty Kaylee."

"And Sadie?"

Betty Lou shifted in her chair. "Sadie was … well … plain Sadie."

CHAPTER ELEVEN

It was a few minutes past two when I left Betty Lou's house. We had exchanged phone numbers, and she promised to let me know when it'd be a good time to come back and talk to Mary Belle and Sadie.

I drove back down to the end of the driveway, stopping at the road. The choices at the moment were to go see Luke or to go have lunch. So far, I'd had coffee and a sweet cinnamon bun today. What I hadn't had was a proper breakfast. If I went to talk to Luke now, I'd probably be hungry before I was done. I headed to Dave's Place.

I had my pick of parking spaces at this time of day, after the lunch crowd had dispersed. I looked for the deputies' car, but it wasn't parked in front of the restaurant entrance, which dashed my slim hope of seeing them again and maybe talking about Kaylee's death. I scanned the lot to be sure before walking in.

I didn't have to stand long by the "Please wait to be seated" sign before the hostess came. I asked for the counter, pointing to where I had sat before, and she seated me, dropping the menu in front of me. I flipped it over, searching for breakfast items. Seeing the headline "Breakfast All Day" brought on a grin. Made my day.

"Hey, hon. What can I get you?"

I looked up, recognizing the waitress I had seen yesterday. "Coffee, please. And an order of scrambled eggs and heavy grits."

She put in the order and returned with a full mug. "Freshly brewed," she said.

"Thank you." I took a sip. Not great, but definitely not lousy. I was a sucker for a good cup of coffee any time of the day. This tasted better than standard restaurant fare.

"Eve ... right?" the waitress said, her cheerful singsong voice matching the upturned smile on her perky face.

I marveled at the effortless way she recalled my name. My eyes darted to her name tag. "You got that right, Caitlin. You know everyone's names here?"

"Not everyone. Most of my customers are regulars, locals. But I get a fair number of travelers coming through," she said as she moved away down the counter, filling more coffee cups.

The ding of a bell coming from the kitchen interrupted my thoughts as I sipped my drink. Caitlin came back with a plateful of steaming food—creamy grits piled high, slabs of melting butter on top, snaking their way down and across the clusters of fluffy eggs, the buttery stream spreading perilously to the rim of the plate.

I dived into my food as if I were starving. Which I was. I had a healthy appetite. When I finished and pushed my plate aside, Caitlin appeared again.

I licked my lips.

"That good, huh?" she asked.

"Perfect," I said, grinning like a Cheshire cat.

"So you stayed?" She leaned forward, her waist pressed against the counter.

"Yup, I'm at the motel across the street. I was really lucky and got the last room there."

She nodded. "We get business from them, and they from us. It works out both ways."

Caitlin filled my coffee mug, cleared my plate, and came back with a towel. She wiped the counter in front of me, keeping her eyes down, seemingly intent on a certain spot, lingering and rewiping over the same area.

At first, I thought it was a stubborn stain or a piece of dried food stuck on the surface, but the area she had rewiped was clean. Then it occurred to me she might be too polite to ask why I was staying.

"I help solve murders," I blurted out.

She looked up, eyebrows raised. Her curiosity unmasked.

I nodded.

She stared at me, a kind of funny look, as if trying to decide whether to believe me.

I hadn't bragged about myself or what I'd done. "Oh wait," I said, remembering I had brought a clipping of the *Prospect* newspaper article home to show my mom. Was it still in my purse? I zipped it open and searched inside, finding it. I handed it to her.

Caitlin reached for it, opening the paper. After she finished reading, she folded it up slowly and gave it back to me. "So you're looking into Kaylee's death?" she asked, the flat tone of her voice bringing it back to the present and straightforward out in the open.

I cast a glance at her solemn face, weighing her question before I answered. "I've given it a lot of thought and decided to stay for a few days. See what I can find out." I quickly brought Caitlin up to speed on my visit to Kaylee's roadside memorial, meeting Lance there, going to Mary Belle's place, and talking to Betty Lou.

She listened earnestly, not interrupting me. "Anything I can do to help?" she asked finally when I was done.

I dug into my purse and pulled out my pen and a notepad. "I'll write my phone number. Call me if you have news?"

"Yeah." She paused, then said in a whisper, "I overheard something when the deputies were talking." She looked around nervously. "This goes nowhere. What I tell you can't be repeated, okay?"

"Okay."

"So they're investigating this road accident, right? But they were saying something about a suspicious death. Maybe a hit and run."

"Did they mention any details?"

She shook her head. "I couldn't hear. They were whispering, and I didn't want to be too obvious."

"Thanks," I said. "Anyone else I should talk to here?"

"Dave Madlin."

"Dave?" I frowned, wondering how he fit in.

"He's the owner. You know ... Dave's Place."

I was slow in connecting all the dots. Dave. The restaurant was named after him. Maybe I was missing something else. "Okay, but what's he got to do with Kaylee?"

"Well, she worked here part time."

"How long ago?"

"Until the end."

"Is he here?"

"I saw him leave earlier. The cook said Dave left to meet with someone."

I made a mental note to check in with Dave later.

"Did Kaylee have any issues here?"

Caitlin looked away and frowned. "I can't be sure ... but I think there's been squabbles over a big-time tipper."

"A customer?"

"Yeah. First time he came in, she was the one who'd waited on him. He sat down at a table, ordered, and ate. Didn't leave nothin' on the table."

"You saw him leave without tipping?"

She shook her head. "One of the other waitresses thought he'd run off without paying. But Kaylee said he palmed money in her hand. She never said how much, even when they asked, and that got everyone curious. It was unusual. There was a bit of competition, and the girls talked. After that, whenever he came back, he made sure to sit at her table."

"Was she okay with it?"

"I think he may have said somethin' to her. She didn't act surprised. We thought she knew he would ask for her again."

"She didn't have to fight off the other girls?"

"Another waitress tried. She had a go with Kaylee. Looked like they were fighting over him."

"Then what happened?"

"I think someone went to get Dave. He came out and broke up the fight. Kaylee got called into his office."

"What did he say to her?"

"I heard he got Kaylee to agree to take turns with the other waitress the next time the big tipper comes back. He's good at this. Anyway, it worked. The two girls made up, and they went back to work."

"The other waitress—what's her name?"

"Debbie."

"Is she here now?"

"No, she's gone."

"Gone?"

"She doesn't work here anymore."

"Know where she went?"

"Nope."

"What can you tell me about her?"

"Well, she'd been working here longer than Kaylee. She's older, maybe late twenties or early thirties."

"Did Kaylee ever fight with you over customers?"

"No, I mainly work at the counter."

My eyes darted left, shooting a pointed glance at the empty stools where the deputies had sat yesterday.

She caught my drift. "They were here early today."

I nodded.

Caitlin lowered her voice again. "They found something out about the nine-one-one call."

My body tensed. "What did the caller say?"

"I don't know."

"Who was it?"

"It was an anonymous call. A male voice. He could be a passerby who did the Good Samaritan thing and reported it." Caitlin's eyes widened as another thought crossed her mind. "Or ... maybe he could be the hit-and-run driver."

CHAPTER TWELVE

It was late in the afternoon when I left Dave's Place. The sun was beating down relentlessly, the temperature at its zenith. Sweat broke out the instant I stepped out of the air-conditioned diner.

I dashed to my ratty old car and drove with the windows slightly open, hoping the breeze would offer a brief respite before the air conditioner kicked in.

Next stop was Luke's house. I was curious about him and his relationship with Kaylee. Maybe he could shed light on this.

I pulled into the driveway, parked behind a dusty sedan, and knocked on the door. I waited. My impatience grew as the sweat poured down my forehead. Hearing nothing, I pounded on the door, irritated at the delay.

It took a while before a young man wearing tattered jeans and a wrinkled T-shirt opened it. He stood in the doorway, barefoot, blinking in the bright sunlight as if he'd just woken up, his sandy-brown hair a disheveled mess.

"Who're you?" he mumbled, squinting.

"Eve Sawyer," I said. "Are you Luke? Lance gave me this address."

He grimaced and rubbed his temples. "He ain't here."

"Oh." I looked around, resigned to the fact that I'd struck out again. "When will he be back?"

"After he gets off work."

I shuffled my feet, feeling let down. "How long will that be?"

"Soon."

I could barely contain my joy at this good news, saving me from having to leave and come back another day.

"It's hot," I blurted out. "I'll have to sit there with the AC running." I pointed to my car.

The guy craned his neck and glanced over my shoulder toward the driveway. He rubbed his eyes.

I felt the prick of a mosquito sting and instinctively slapped my neck, making a sharp, loud sound. "Er, mind if I wait inside?"

He shook his head as if he had made a decision. "Come in," he grunted, pushing the door open wider and stepping back to give me more room.

I moved quickly, walking past him as he closed the door. The air was marginally cooler in the living room, where the AC window unit was running.

I looked around the small room. An unpretentious TV on the wall, a plain floor lamp, a messy coffee table placed in front of a chunky sofa. He gestured to it—the thick, sagging cushions had seen finer days.

"Thank you." I smiled as I sat down. "And you're Luke's friend?"

"Mike," he said as he shuffled, dragging his feet to the other end of the sofa and slumping onto it.

I checked the time on my phone. "So Luke is getting off work? Did he say he'll be coming here right after?"

"Yeah."

"Have you known him long?"

"Yeah."

"You have family here?"

Mike looked down, slurring, "No, my parents are dead."

"I'm sorry." I shifted in my seat, wishing I hadn't brought up the subject. He seemed to be having a difficult time. I felt ashamed of thinking he was lazy when I saw his drowsy appearance at the door and mistook it for idleness.

I quickly dismissed my mistaken thought and curtailed my curiosity and further questions as I killed time, rifling through magazines on the coffee table. Seeing a stunning model on the cover of a women's fashion magazine, I picked it up and flipped it open, wondering if it was Kaylee's. A slim, flat hair clip slipped out, falling into the crack between the sofa cushions. I slid my hand down there and touched something small and hard. When I pulled it out and held it in the palm of my hand, I saw it was a small flower with rhinestones in the petals. I heard the click of a key in the lock and quickly shoved it back when the front door opened.

I didn't know who was more surprised—me or the tall young man looming in the doorway.

Mike broke the awkward moment and quickly introduced us. Luke had an athletic build, like he could have played football as a quarterback. He was quick with a smile as he crossed the room to meet me. "Hi, Eve," he said, gesturing for me to sit back down as I got up. "So what brings you out here?"

"I'm sorry to hear about Kaylee."

He frowned. "Did you know her?"

"No." I paused briefly. "I was at Dave's Place when I first heard. Then I saw it on the news."

A vacant look passed over his face, and his eyes stared into the distance.

"I'm sorry," I whispered as the mention of Kaylee brought this change in Luke. Lance had said they'd been close, but later broke up. Apparently, he still had feelings for her and was likely grieving her death.

He sighed.

I spoke softly and quickly, giving him a quick recap leading up to the present, then showed him the newspaper article and told him why I had stayed and why I was at his house.

Luke didn't interrupt me. When I finished, he asked, "Are you sure about doing this?"

"My mind's made up," I said.

A flicker crossed his face, an unspoken response, as if he shared the certainty of my conviction.

"You guys broke up, right?" I asked.

"We had argued." He heaved a sigh.

"Why?"

"Kaylee was headstrong. Wanted to do things her way. I didn't see things the same. We started fighting more and more."

"What did you fight about?"

"Kaylee wanted to leave."

"Leave town?"

"Yup, leave town. Leave me." He gave a sharp laugh. "It all amounted to the same. She accused me of holding her back, of standing in her way. Things got heated. I knew if we kept on, one of us would say something we'd both really regret."

"So you broke up with her, or she broke up with you?"

"We both did." He grunted. "That's the only thing we agreed on."

"When was this?"

"A couple months ago."

"Were you bitter?"

"Bitter, mad as hell—you name it."

"Are you still?"

He shook his head.

"Can you think of anyone who would want Kaylee dead?"

He leveled his blue eyes at mine. "That's a loaded question. You've decided it wasn't an accident?"

I stared back. "No," I said, quickly adding, "Of course not."

CHAPTER THIRTEEN

A QUICK GLANCE AT THE DASHBOARD SHOWED MY TANK was a quarter full. I had let it go to empty once, driving on the sheer belief there were a couple of residual gallons in the tank after the needle pointed to E. I learned that lesson the hard way. I'd never let my tank get below a quarter since.

I remembered passing a gas station on the way to Luke's about a mile back.

It was a small, forlorn-looking structure with two pumps. I pulled up to the first one, got out of my car, and unscrewed the gas cap. The pump had a "Pay Inside First" sign. I stepped inside, opening a door marred by dirt and smudged fingerprints. It was quiet, with no cars whizzing by on the road. I was the only customer. No clerk at the worn checkout counter. An antique oil can sat at the far side of it next to a couple of red gas cans and miscellaneous car items.

"Hello?" I called out. It was eerily silent. I cleared my throat and yelled, "Anyone here?"

A door shut in the distance, and an old man emerged, shuffling to the counter, his tired face lined with the years of hard living, his body worn down with pain or the drudgery of life, or maybe both.

I regretted the harshness of my voice, the echoes reverberating in my mind. "I'm sorry," I said with an apologetic smile.

He looked at me, a glint of a sparkle in his dull eyes. "Traveling through?"

My smile widened in a warm greeting.

He opened and closed his mouth as if he had something to say and thought better of it.

"I'm Eve," I said. "I'm sticking around here for a few days. I've got some time before school starts."

"Taking a vacation?"

"That was my original plan, but the tragedy here, Kaylee…"

His lips quivered.

"Did you know her?"

"Yeah," he muttered.

"I'm trying to find out what happened to her. I'm a journalism student at Midway College."

He frowned. "We're so small, we don't even have our own police or fire department. We rely on the county sheriff. They're working on the case."

"I'm not here in an official capacity." I pulled out the creased newspaper article and gave it to him to read.

He looked up when he was done. "You did good."

I hid my blush, ducking my head to tuck the paper back in my purse. "Were you working here that night?"

"No, I've been closing early."

"Why?"

"Business has been slow."

I nodded.

"Don't make sense to hire somebody to stay late."

"Do you have a pay phone?"

He thumbed, pointing outside.

"Security camera work?" I tilted my head toward the store front, where I'd noticed one.

"It's fickle sometimes. The sheriff's department asked me. I've got someone looking at it."

"If it's working, call me." I gave him my number, then grabbed a pack of peanut butter crackers and soda, paid for them and the gas, finished pumping, and went back to the motel, calling it an early night.

CHAPTER FOURTEEN

I woke up with the bright sunlight streaming in my motel window. I squinted, casting my eyes toward a torn plastic wrapper and cracker crumbs that had scattered on the covers. I fell back on the bed, recalling that I'd been exhausted and passed out the night before on top of the covers with my clothes on and the curtains partially drawn.

I yawned, stretching and checking the time—7:36 a.m.

My mouth was dry. I had fallen asleep without brushing my teeth. My clothes looked rumpled and dirty. I swung my legs over the bed and ran to the bathroom to clean up and shower.

Dressed in a fresh T-shirt, jeans, and socks, I hastily towel-dried my hair as thoughts of breakfast at Dave's diner across the road entered my mind. My stomach growled, a reminder of the meager crackers that had served as a poor substitute for a meal last night. I grabbed my purse, opened the door, and rushed out.

I had parked my car in front of my motel room, facing the door. The sight that met my eyes brought me to a full stop. I blinked, my mouth falling open.

A sudden feeling of icy dread filled my chest.

I placed a hand on the car hood, steadying my shaky legs as I stared at the menacing bright red messages spray-painted on my windshield and side windows: "Get out!" "Leave town now!"

Who would do this?

I took a step back and scrutinized my vandalized car. The front tire on the passenger side had deflated. I circled around to check the other three tires and saw the front driver's side tire was also flat. I bent down for a closer inspection and noticed someone had slashed those two tires.

I looked around the motel lot, but I didn't see anyone. It was quiet; the serenity of early morning accompanied the chirping of birds.

I checked the other cars in the parking lot. No one graffitied or vandalized them.

The motel office was dark; a reversible "Closed" sign hung in the window.

Propelled by a rush of adrenaline and anger, I raced across the road to Dave's Place. I saw the sheriff's department car parked in front of the door.

I went inside, bypassing the hostess in the front, and made a beeline to the counter, where the deputies were seated in their usual place.

Caitlin was talking to them, laughing as she filled their coffee mugs. They had finished their meals, their plates pushed aside. She looked up as I approached; her face stiffened in mid-laughter. "What's wrong, hon?"

I slid into the seat next to the deputies and pointed to her carafe. "Coffee, please."

She quickly filled my mug. I grasped it with both hands and sipped.

Caitlin was watching me. "Are you okay?"

I took a deep breath, letting out a sigh. My heartbeat slowed. I'd gotten a grip now.

"What happened?" she asked again, speaking loud enough to alert the sheriff's deputies who were sitting right there. I had their attention as they turned to stare at me and listen.

"My car got vandalized."

"Where did this happen?" the older of the two deputies asked.

"At the Pines Motel," I said. "Someone spray-painted my car and slashed my front tires."

"Who would do that?" Caitlin asked.

"I don't know. But whoever it was left threatening messages."

"What messages?" the younger deputy sitting next to me cut in. He wore a badge and name tag that said "Clark."

"Get out. Leave town now," I answered.

"We need to see this," the older deputy said. His badge said "Wilson." "We'll take our coffees to go," he told Caitlin.

"Mine too, please," I said.

CHAPTER FIFTEEN

I walked back to the Pines Motel while the deputies got in their car and drove there. Caitlin had shoved a brown paper sack in my hand as I left. I opened it, giving a grateful smile as I pulled out a warm egg sandwich. By the time I reached my car, I had gobbled my sandwich and washed it down with the coffee.

The deputies were busy examining my car and already taking photos. They asked me questions. I gave my statement and contact information. They didn't act surprised when I brought up Kaylee and explained she was the reason I stayed in town. Caitlin probably mentioned that to them already. They had seen me at Dave's before. It was their business to know. To their credit, they didn't discourage me, but they cautioned me about safety. They gave me the sheriff's office number to call anytime, and another one for a garage with a tow service. It was the only one closest to this place.

I heard the distant slam of a car door and running footsteps.

"Hey, what's going on?" asked the guy as he rushed up, panting. I recognized MC, the clerk from the motel.

"Did you see this vandalism?" Deputy Clark asked.

MC blinked, taking in the graffiti scrawled on my car. He cursed and shook his head.

"What time did you leave?"

"Huh ... me?" He paused. "When the office closed."

"Don't you have an overnight clerk?"

"No, sir."

"When did you leave?"

"Around ten, I guess."

"You don't know?"

"Yeah, yeah," MC said. "I stay past, you know, some-times, and sometimes I—"

"Leave early?"

He nodded.

"So you were gone sometime around ten until"—Clark looked at his watch—"around eight-thirty this morning."

"Yes, sir."

"Do the cameras work?" Deputy Clark asked.

"Off and on." MC shrugged. "I'll have to find out."

"We'll also need the names of the guests staying here."

"I'll get you the info," MC said as he led the deputies inside the motel.

I STAYED OUTSIDE by my car and called the garage. I checked the time and figured I might be their first customer since it probably just opened. When a man answered, I explained the situation and what I needed, mentioning that the sheriff had referred me to their business. That got the guy's attention. Before we were done talking, he was already on his way.

This would set me back financially. I had managed to live within my means, balancing student financial aid from grants and loans, a scholarship, and work-study income with frugal living and careful budgeting. I'd accumulated some small savings for emergencies with the little money I'd set aside each month. In some months, I saved a hundred dollars, others, only ten dollars. Every dollar had counted, and my little savings grew. I had my mom to thank for that. A single mom who raised me and gave me the best life she could, filled with lots of love and hopes for the future. I watched as she sacrificed, struggled, and prayed for me. She instilled in me independence and strength, and a strong sense of justice and what was right and wrong.

It wasn't long before the guy from the garage arrived, introducing himself as Daniel. He examined my car before hooking on the tow chains. I asked him about the cost of the tow and fixing the two damaged tires.

He gave me an estimate, which included the tow, a set of two new tires mounted and balanced, and the disposal fee for my old ones. The look on my face must have told him that the quote was more than I expected. "I can order those, or you may want to get used tires," he said. "I don't know if we have those tires lying around, but I'll check for you and let you know."

I nodded.

"In a hurry to get back on the road?"

"No."

He raised his eyebrows. "So when do you need this done?"

"As soon as possible."

"As soon as possible," he repeated slowly.

I swallowed. "This vandalism ... has caught me by surprise." Sensing his concern was genuine, and also his curiosity, I told him, "Initially I was passing through, taking a trip away to relax before school started. But when I heard about Kaylee, I couldn't leave without looking into her death. I'm a journalism student and have some experience investigating murders."

"But wasn't Kaylee's death an accident?" he said.

"That may be, but it hasn't been ruled yet."

"And you think it may be—"

I shook my head. "It's too early to tell." I gestured toward my car. "I've poked around and talked to people, but now this—this was no accident."

Before he left, Daniel offered to remove the graffiti.

"I could do it," I said, "with the right stuff and elbow grease."

He waved it off. "No charge. I'll take care of it."

I smiled and thanked him for his unexpected act of kindness to a stranger.

CHAPTER SIXTEEN

THE EMPTY PARKING SPACE IN FRONT OF MY MOTEL
room set a dismal tone. I missed my car. I allowed
myself a moment of sadness before I seethed with
indignation. Who inflicted this damage on my car? And
why had they done this?

I went into my room to think. I clenched my fist. It
wouldn't be so easy to get rid of me. I was determined
before, and now, more so. That it had happened to me
now could mean whoever did it was still here in town.

I paced the small room from the bathroom to the
bed and back, thinking about the problem with my car
and the temporary impediment of not having a means
of transportation, the unexpected financial burden, and
the delay in looking into Kaylee's death.

On the third loop around, I stopped, grabbed my
phone, and sat down on the bed. I checked my bank
account first. Working from the balance and Daniel's
estimate, I calculated my expenses. New tires would

take precious money out of my savings, cutting close to my comfort level. The motel stay would be shorter, based on my budget. And that meant I'd have to leave town early.

Kaylee's case was paramount, and I couldn't drop that and leave. Right now, buying used tires made more sense, and with the considerable savings, I could afford to stay longer. I didn't see any way around it.

I picked up my cell phone and dialed the garage.

"Hey, I was just about to call you," Daniel said when he answered. I could hear the excitement in his voice, the upbeat sound.

"I have good news for you," he blurted. "I checked on your tires and found two used ones in good condition, at a fraction of the cost of new tires."

"Oh, that's fantastic!" I said, overjoyed to hear this.

"I can put them on your car. Does that work for you?"

"Yes, please go ahead."

"We'll get your car done today. Can you come to the garage this afternoon?"

"What time?"

"Get here by four thirty. We close at five."

"Okay. I'll be there." I hung up the call with a sigh of relief.

CHAPTER SEVENTEEN

THE MOTEL PARKING LOT WAS CLEAR EXCEPT FOR TWO vehicles now. One was a grungy old car parked by the office, its dark reddish-brown color faded and dull. I recalled that it was parked in the same spot when MC checked me in. My guess was it was his vehicle. The other car was a dusty black four-door sedan parked about two doors down from the office.

I took a leisurely walk and peeked in the window of Room 5. Someone had drawn back the curtains on both sides, made the bed, removed the trash, and straightened the small round table and chair. Everything looked neat and in place, ready for the next guest. Room 4 looked the same. But in Room 3, someone had only partially drawn the curtains. Through the sunlit opening, I could see the unmade bed, rumpled pillows, and overflowing trash can. On the table next to the window were lipstick-smeared cups and takeout containers. No one appeared to be in. As I passed by the last two rooms, a quick glance showed they were ready for guests.

When I entered the motel office, MC looked up from where he sat behind the counter, his eyes registering a greeting.

"Hi," I said.

He tilted his head. "You okay?"

I nodded, resting my arms on the counter. "Did you notice anything last night?"

"Me? No."

"You left around ten?"

"Yep."

"What about the other guests?"

"Two of them checked out early. Left their keys in the night box."

"Do you think they had anything to do with it?"

"I doubt it. They were traveling together. Two families. Spent one night here, and they left early this morning."

"And the others?"

"We have a couple with a child who are still here."

"Looks like they're in Room 3," I said, wondering if they saw or heard anything.

MC nodded.

"What about the other two rooms?"

"They were unoccupied last night."

I thought about the other guests. I had focused my attention on the people in town, the ones I had talked to, but not the other people staying here.

I thought about my dwindling savings. That

reminded me of another reason I needed to see MC—a financial matter. I gulped, feeling uneasy about how much longer I could afford to stay at the motel, knowing what I had to do. "I'd like to book another night, please."

He grinned from ear to ear, baring his teeth. I blinked, noticing for the first time how straight they were and how different he looked, how handsome.

"We have a special going on now. Stay three nights, get one night free."

"Really?" I brightened up, wanting to be assured I had heard him correctly.

"Yes, ma'am. Would you like that?"

"I'll take it! Thank you!" I squealed. Pay for one more night, and the fourth night was free. Was I lucky or what? I didn't know if MC had somehow done this to help me out, but I was grateful. I'd still have money left after the next two nights if needed.

CHAPTER EIGHTEEN

It was mid-afternoon. I checked the map on my phone app to get directions to the service garage. It was just over a mile from the Pines Motel. It was a blazing-hot day, the sun beating down mercilessly, not a cloud in the sky. Normally, it would take me about twenty minutes to walk that far, but I wanted to take it easy. I straightened my clothes and stretched my legs. I had plenty of time to get there, even walking at a leisurely pace.

I stayed on the shoulder of the roadway, away from the heated asphalt, and as close as I could get under the shaded areas where forest trees lined the road—a mixture of mostly pine and oak, and some hickory or beech.

My travel path wasn't straight or level, and there was banking where the road curved. I trudged along, stepping carefully on the uneven surfaces, avoiding rocks and ditches and clumps of weeds. Occasionally, I kicked a pebble, bouncing it out over the path.

I didn't mind the walk; it gave me time to ponder and reflect.

Whoever had tried to frighten me away didn't succeed. It had the opposite effect. More than ever, I was determined to find out what happened to Kaylee. Why would anyone go to this trouble if her death was an accident? They treated me as someone who posed a risk to them. They wanted to get rid of me. Maybe they read the newspaper articles about me. Maybe they knew I was someone to contend with, even though I didn't wear a badge. I sure didn't look like one—me, a slim twenty-one-year-old tawny-haired college student.

VAIN WAS SO SMALL, it didn't have a main street. It was barely a dot on the map. The few businesses were scattered. I could see why it took a drive to the next closest town, Bearsville, to get things. After more than half an hour, I arrived at Daniel's Garage, marked by a sign fixed over the door. It was on a corner lot at an intersection. Several cars were parked off to the side.

I hurried across the stained concrete pad to the small office, my shoes scraping on the hard surface. Inside, the blast of cool air-conditioning clashed with my sweat-dampened clothes. I shivered at the sudden change in temperature as I looked around the cramped, grimy room. A messy counter on one end, three well-worn chairs for customers in the office/waiting area, a plain table with a coffee station, a drip coffee pot on and stacked paper cups turned upside down.

There was no one here, but through the glass side door connecting to the garage, I could see Daniel working on my car which was lifted up in the bay. It looked like a one-mechanic auto shop.

I took a seat and waited. I had come early.

The ringing phone startled me. After the third ring, I wondered if Daniel would stop working to answer. The side door flung open, and a young teenage-looking boy rushed in and picked up the phone. I listened to his one-sided conversation and gathered a customer was calling. With the confirmation of "it's ready," the kid hung up the phone, throwing a glance my way.

"Hi," I said.

"Oh, I didn't hear you come in." He squinted at the parked cars outside.

"I walked." I smiled at the kid, noting a resemblance to the mechanic. "I'm Eve. My car is—"

"Oh, I know which one. My dad told me." He shook his head. "That sucks, what happened."

"You're—"

"Rob," he said, beaming. "Your car will be ready soon. He's almost finished with your tires."

"Great," I said.

"Look over this and sign." He slid over a sheet of paper.

Everything looked fine on the invoice, with used

tires just like Daniel had stated. I signed and paid with my credit card.

Rob handed me a receipt. "He's pulling your car out now."

"You're his assistant?"

He straightened up, thrusting his chest out. "Yes, ma'am. I work here during the summer. And in the afternoons during the school year."

"Well, I'm glad to meet you."

I heard a car driving up and doors slamming. The office door swung open, and in walked two guys. I recognized them immediately.

Mike came in first and headed straight for the counter. He spoke to Rob, who showed him some paperwork, and then he reached for his wallet to square up his bill.

Meanwhile, Luke hung back to wait and smiled when he saw me walking toward him. "What're you doing here, Eve?"

"My car was vandalized."

His eyes widened as he drew in his breath sharply.

"Someone slashed the front tires and sprayed graffiti on my car."

"Did you call the police?"

"I spoke to the sheriff's deputies who were eating at Dave's Place, and they came out to investigate."

"Man, I'm sorry," he said, lowering his voice. "If there's anything I can do to help…"

"Daniel's fixing my car. I'm here to pick it up."

We paused as Mike turned around and walked back to us, paperwork in hand. "I'm all set. Let's go eat."

Luke glanced at the rustic wooden wall clock showing a quarter to five and then at me. "Free for dinner?"

I nodded, realizing I had eaten nothing all day except for the egg sandwich this morning.

"How about we head over to Dave's Place?"

"Meet you there," I said.

CHAPTER NINETEEN

Dave's Place was not bustling yet when we arrived. Luke got us a booth in the back, which was relatively quiet. Despite the worn-out condition of the fake leather seats, it was comfortable, the stiffness having loosened.

Luke and Mark didn't need menus, giving their orders of iced teas and hamburger steaks with mashed potatoes and gravy and green beans as soon as the waitress arrived. I ordered from the menu a plate of four veggies, a roll, and coffee.

We got our drinks promptly and made small talk while waiting for our food.

A few minutes later, our food arrived, steaming hot and piled high. The waitress was businesslike and efficient—no wasted time or chitchat. She put a bottle of steak sauce on the table, her alert eyes scanning our plates like a professional. "Need anything else?"

"No, thank you," we said, answering simultaneously.

I noticed her name tag, Doreen, and gray-streaked hair neatly pulled back in a bun. Yes, I would like something else, but it wasn't food. I shook my head as she retreated. I stuck my fork in a heap of juicy green beans on my plate as a growl emanated from my belly.

The diner had signs advertising home-cooked meals and locally farmed produce. The food wasn't fancy, but it sure was delicious. I hadn't always been a vegetarian, but when I made the choice, it was a conscious, ethical decision—one that I'd never regretted. I didn't judge others for their choices, and I held on to mine. But occasionally, the tantalizing smell and sound of sizzling bacon still tempted me—almost, but never.

Luke, Mike, and I made haste with our food, finishing within minutes of each other. I wiped my lips with the paper napkin and sat back, gulping the rest of my coffee. I regretted not savoring my dinner, but hunger drove me to it.

Doreen reappeared and refilled our drinks without us having to wave her over. "Enjoy your dinner?" she asked, with a hint of a smile on her lips.

"Compliments to the chef." I returned her smile.

"I will let him know," she said. "Would you like dessert? We have homemade pies and cakes."

Luke flashed a wolfish grin. Yup, I bet he'd had them all. "What do you suggest?" I asked him.

"I'm a pie guy—the key lime pie."

"I'll have the key lime pie too," I said.

Doreen winked at us, then turned to Mike. "So just two orders?"

"Hey, make it three," he said.

"You got it." She wrote down our orders and turned to go.

"Oh wait," I called out. "Is Dave Madlin here tonight by any chance?"

She took a step back and wrinkled her brow. "Is there a problem?"

"No, not at all. Can you please see if he'd talk to me tonight?"

"And who are you?"

"Eve Sawyer. I'm a journalism student. I was passing through town when I heard about Kaylee's death. The other waitress, Caitlin, told me she had worked here."

Doreen stared at me, paling, a blank look on her face.

"I'm so sorry." My hand flew up to cover my mouth. "You must have known her. Worked with her."

Her chin trembled. She pressed her hands on the table to steady herself.

"Would you like some water?" I lifted my water glass, which I had not touched.

Doreen shook her head, whispering that she was going to the bathroom to compose herself.

"Where do I find Dave?"

She pointed to his office. "I'm going that way."

I got up and followed her, passing the bathroom on my way to the room at the end of the hall to see him.

Dave's office door was ajar. Through the opening, I

could see the corner of a desk stacked with paper. I knocked gently.

"Come in," a hearty masculine voice called out.

A handsome, silver-haired man, probably in his late fifties or early sixties, peered at me through rectangular bifocals as I walked in. He was sitting at a massive oak desk, going over paperwork and what looked like receipts, with piles of paper arranged in neat stacks on the side.

"Hope I'm not interrupting—"

He raised his eyebrows. "Is this important?"

"Yes," I said. "I'm Eve Sawyer, a journalism student. I'd like to ask you some questions ... about Kaylee. I understand she worked here."

He scrutinized me with kind eyes that bore a glimmer of sadness, then eased back in his squeaky wooden chair and gestured to the straight-backed chair facing him.

I sat and pulled out the crinkled newspaper article. "This will tell you a bit more about me."

He read the article, looking up and down at the newspaper photo and then at me. "Eve Sawyer," he said in a voice tinged with respect.

I flushed and dropped my gaze, landing on the solid wood block with his brass nameplate on his desk, facing me. "I'd like your help, Mr. Madlin."

He chuckled. "Call me Dave. Everyone else does."

"Okay, Dave." I laughed.

"Now, how can I help you?"

"I'd like to get a sense of Kaylee's character. What kind of person she was."

"She was an outstanding employee. Reliable. Worked when she was scheduled. Rarely called in sick."

"How was she with the customers?"

"She was a popular waitress. I didn't get any complaints—except once."

I sat up, ears perked. "What happened?"

"There was some ruckus over a big tipper. Another waitress thought she was greedy, staking her claim on him like he was her exclusive customer."

"I heard it was Debbie. Was it her?"

Dave paused, studying me as if he were deciding what to answer or how much to tell me. Then he leaned forward. "What I'm going to tell you is what Kaylee confided in me. This customer ... him being a big tipper. Caitlin had needled her about this guy endlessly, wanting to know about her tips. The truth was this guy left no tips. He told her he had forgotten his wallet and said that he'd make it up to her. But when Caitlin persisted, Kaylee blurted out that he was a big tipper. Kaylee was kindhearted and wanted to protect his dignity. But it backfired. Caitlin spread the word and fanned envy and rivalry among the other waitresses and damaged Kaylee's reputation. Even when Kaylee told her the truth and asked Caitlin to stop, she didn't."

"Why did Caitlin do that?"

"She was jealous of Kaylee. Younger, prettier, and a more popular waitress."

"So what did you do?"

"After I talked to each of them, I separated their workstations. Sent Caitlin to work behind the counter, and Kaylee to her station on the floor."

I nodded, thinking back to what Caitlin had told me. What Dave said made sense and shone a light on the truth. I thought of something else to ask him. "But who trained Kaylee? Surely it wasn't Caitlin." I had an inkling of the answer, but I wanted to find out from Dave.

"Doreen did. She took her under her wing."

"She was our waitress tonight. She's still all shook up and grieving."

"Doreen is older, and not like the other girls. She's not gossipy. I think Kaylee trusted her," Dave said as he handed back the newspaper article. "She could probably tell you more about Kaylee."

"Thank you, Dave." I smiled, pushing back my chair and standing up. "I appreciate your time and help."

I stopped by the bathroom to check on Doreen. Inside, I saw two rustic wooden vanities with round sinks. She was standing in front of one, facing a mirror, dabbing away tears with a tissue.

I moved closer to stand next to her, by the other vanity.

Doreen looked like she'd aged, her face sagging and eyes lackluster. She'd let go of her businesslike facade and any pretense of a brave front.

"I know it's been hard," I said.

She turned her face away.

I glanced at the two stalls, ducking down and checking to make sure no one else was in here. "Were you working with Kaylee the night she died?"

Doreen nodded, staring down.

"Did she say or do anything different that night?"

She cleared her throat. I waited, but she didn't talk.

"Look, I know you were close, and Kaylee trusted you."

She burst into tears.

I handed her a tissue from the dispenser on the vanity. Then another one. And waited a moment before I asked, "When did the diner close?"

"Ten." She sniffed and reached out for another tissue.

"You both left at that time?"

"No, we were supposed to stay and close up. But Kaylee had been acting impatient and repeatedly checking her phone and the time."

"Did you know why?"

"I asked her, and she said she had something to do after work."

"She didn't say what it was?"

"Nope. But I knew it was something important. I offered to help." Doreen smiled briefly. "I told her to go, and that I'd close up. You should've seen the look of relief on her face."

"You were a good friend."

"That's what she said. Then she hugged me. Said she was meeting someone she'd met at the diner."

"A man or woman?"

"My guess, it was a man. Kaylee brought a change of clothing with her to work. I watched her go into the bathroom after her shift. She switched out of her waitress outfit and fixed her hair real nice and put on fresh makeup. Oh, and she showed off her pretty rhinestone flower sandals. Said they were brand new." Doreen had a faraway look in her eyes. "She looked gorgeous from head to toe. You should've seen her."

"She didn't appear worried or apprehensive?"

"Not at all."

"Was she excited?"

"Oh yeah. Like she couldn't wait to see him."

"You helped her."

A grim look changed Doreen's expression. "Helped her or …?"

CHAPTER TWENTY

I MADE MY WAY BACK TO THE TABLE. LUKE AND MIKE had finished their dessert, their plates cleared away. Luke pointed to my slice of key lime pie and made a thumbs-up gesture.

"You had a good talk?" Mike asked as I sat down.

"Yeah, sorry it took so long."

"It's okay, Luke and I are just chatting."

"About what?" I asked.

"My car."

"Oh, I wondered about that," I said, recalling there was a dusty car in their driveway yesterday. "Was it a big job?"

"No, just a check," Mike said. "I ran into a tree."

"That sounds major," I said.

"Not that bad—dents, scratches on the bumper. Took it in for Daniel to check it over."

"That's reassuring," I said, nodding and eyeing the

generous slice of chilled pie. "He took care of my car too."

I took a bite of the pie. "Mmm, so delicious," I mumbled, closing my eyes to enjoy how good it tasted.

"Hey, what's going on?" Mike cried sharply.

My eyes flew open at the sound of his cry, seeing the confused look on his face and unease. And perhaps hearing fear in his voice. The two sheriff's deputies were standing by our table, one on each side of him.

"Please come with us, Mike," Wilson said.

"Why?" His eyes darted frantically. "Are you arresting me?"

"We'd like you to come with us."

My mouth dropped open. I was at a loss for words. Was Mike a suspect? Or a person of interest? Did this have anything to do with his car?

"We'd like to ask you some questions at the station. Please come quietly," Deputy Clark said.

Luke wrapped a protective arm around Mike. "He doesn't have to answer your questions if he's not being arrested. He didn't do anything."

For a moment, there was hushed silence.

"No, I'll go," Mike finally said quietly, rising. He left the diner, sandwiched between the two officers.

I couldn't forget the look on his face.

CHAPTER TWENTY-ONE

That night, I had nightmares.

My terrors heightened. I dreamt of dark shapes creeping around my motel door, jiggling the knob, trying to get in. I had nowhere to run. I was locked in the room. I ran into the bathroom frantically, looking for a way out. There were no windows. I went to the front and peeked out through a crack in the window curtains. Shadows loomed. I whipped my head back and pressed my back to the wall, trembling, listening for a sound.

I heard a faint cry that sounded like, "Help." It was muffled, distant. Then I heard it again—a female voice, low, soft, and gasping.

Then again, I heard the cry for help—this time it was rash, urgent, loaded with adrenaline from every pore of her body, yet choked with desperation and despair.

Then, with a mournful wail, her energy spent, she realized that help would never come.

Then it was a whimper, as if she knew no amount of fight could save her.

As if she were facing a cruel monster that would bring death.

Then it was nothing at all. Only silence.

I woke up in a cold sweat and stumbled to the sink to dash water on my face. I jammed my body against the sink, grabbing on to the sides, staring at my pallid reflection in the mirror.

An indeterminate amount of time passed before I crawled back into bed, tumbling on top of jumbled, twisted sheets. I curled up in a corner, hugging a pillow, until fitful sleep eventually overtook me.

SUNLIGHT FILTERED through the slits in the curtains. I cracked open my eyes and glimpsed my surroundings, thankful I didn't remember the details of my dreams, sensing they had been horrible.

I swung my legs over the bed and got on my knees to check beneath it. Nothing was hiding under the bed except for a few dust bunnies. I looked under the nightstand next to it. It was clear. Satisfied, I used one hand on the mattress to push myself up.

It was then that I glimpsed a piece of white paper, its folded edge hanging in balance on top of the lamp cord plugged into the wall behind the nightstand. I flattened my hand to squeeze it in the narrow space, pinching the paper between my thumb and index finger and pulling it out. I unfolded it. It was a torn-off scrap of paper with a scrawled ten-digit number and a name under it—Jimmy. The digits were grouped and spaced out like a phone number, including the area code. I flipped it over. It was blank on the other side.

Had someone exchanged phone numbers before a date? Was it a call to someone on a lonely night? Someone who never showed up ... the note discarded in disappointment? I slipped it into my purse and walked to the window, drawing the curtains apart.

The morning light suddenly illuminated and bathed the room in its brightness. A beautiful new day was beginning. An uplifting spirit and hope stirred, strengthening me. Reminded me why I was here. Why I stayed. What I must do. Kaylee needed me. I had to continue my search for the truth.

I took a quick shower and dressed in a yellow polka-dotted top and my favorite pair of jeans.

I walked out into the motel lot and to Room 3. The curtains were closed, which was a good sign the guests were still in there. I knocked on the door. Heard some muffled sounds. I rapped again, harder this time. Inside, a woman's voice yelled, "Get the door!"

About a minute later, the door opened. A groggy man in shorts squinted at me with one eye closed.

"Sorry to disturb you," I said, holding up my motel key. "I'm Eve, down at the end."

He grunted, blinking at the bright sunlight.

"Someone vandalized my car yesterday. Did you see anything?"

He tipped his head back and bellowed toward the back of the darkened room, "Her car was vandalized. Anyone see anything suspicious?" I stepped away from the motel door and purposely averted my eyes to give the people inside some privacy. Hearing no response, he turned back to face me. "Nope."

I mumbled a thanks, turning to leave. Then I noticed a black minivan in the parking lot. I paused and pointed to it. "Is that your vehicle?"

The man nodded.

"I remember seeing it when I checked in," I said. "Were you here the night before Kaylee was found dead?"

The man stiffened, staring at me.

Did I touch a raw nerve? "Let me start over. I've been looking into Kaylee's accident, asking questions, talking to people. Then somebody slashed my tires and left a threatening message." I softened my voice as he grew more alert and listened intently. "I'm asking for your help. If you saw anything the night Kaylee died, I need to know, okay?"

He acknowledged me with a slight nod.

"What do you recall that night? Anything, even a minor detail, may be important."

He rubbed his jaw, running his fingers over the shadowy stubble. "We've spoken to the sheriff. My wife and kid, they were asleep in the double bed nearest the bathroom. I had the other double bed in the front all to myself. I was exhausted. Too wiped out to get up and take a shower." He hesitated, pausing. "I suddenly woke up. I don't know what woke me."

"What time was that?"

He knitted his brow. "I think it was sometime late at night. My wife was snoring. The kid was fast asleep. The curtains were drawn except for a tiny gap that was open. I could tell it was pitch-dark outside."

"What happened next?"

"I thought I heard some shouting. Then an engine cutting on, some other noise."

"In the parking lot?"

"Yeah. I wondered who'd be out there."

"Did you see the vehicle?"

"No, I stayed in bed. Didn't feel a need to get up and look."

"Anything else?"

"I drifted in and out of sleep. Then I woke up again later. I heard something again. Door slam. Engine starting. Then the gravel crunching under tires as the vehicle sped away." He scratched his head. "I swear I didn't dream that—it sounded so real."

CHAPTER TWENTY-TWO

I beat the morning crowd at Dave's Place and made a beeline to my usual spot at the counter. I searched for Caitlin. She must have felt my potent gaze, because she stopped chatting with another customer and our eyes made contact.

I sat straight, perched high on my stool, and watched her.

She made her way to me, clutching her order pad. Her lips trembled in a forced smile. "What can I get you today?"

I gave her a curt nod. I needed my caffeine first. "I'll have coffee, black. And an order of eggs and grits."

She put in my order pronto and came back with a steaming mug of coffee. She didn't stay to chat.

That was okay with me. I enjoyed my coffee in peace. It had a settling effect, loosening the tightness and smoothing my edges.

When my food came, I tackled it with zest. As soon

as I finished, Caitlin whisked my plate away and cleared off the counter in front of me.

Except for my coffee mug, which I was holding. "Refill, please," I said.

I waited until she came back with a brimming cup. "Caitlin, we need to talk."

She grabbed her order pad again, holding it against her chest.

I went straight to it. "Did you tell me the truth about Kaylee's big tipper?"

She fidgeted.

"There was no big tipper, was there?"

"That's what she told me," Caitlin said, her eyes flashing in defiance.

"But she told you the truth later and asked you not to spread the rumor, right?"

Her cheeks flushed, and she quickly glanced away.

"And later you elaborated on the story and made up the part about the fight?" I asked.

She licked her lips.

"Did you do that?"

"Yeah."

"So it wasn't true?"

"No," she said, her voice cracking. "But you don't understand how it snowballed. I ... I couldn't stop." Her eyes pleaded with me.

"It hurt Kaylee," I said.

Caitlin's shoulders slumped. "I'm really sorry."

CHAPTER TWENTY-THREE

I MADE A CALL TO LUKE AFTER LEAVING THE DINER. HE
didn't want to talk over the phone, and suggested that I
meet him instead, giving me directions to the farm
where he was working.

It was early in the day, the temperature cool from
the night before. I drove to the farm with the windows
rolled down to let the morning air in.

Luke had told me he'd be outside mending a fence.
He spotted me when I turned onto the gravel driveway
and waved.

I stepped out of my car and stretched, inhaling a
lungful of fresh country air.

"Hey." He set his tools down on the ground and
walked toward me.

"Good morning, Luke."

His smile was strained. It didn't look like he had a
good night's sleep, if the circles under his eyes were
any indication.

"Worried about Mike?" I asked.

He nodded.

"Did they arrest him?"

"No." He sighed. "They let him go, for now."

"Tell me what happened."

Luke ran a hand over his buzz cut. "They took him to the sheriff's office for questioning regarding Kaylee's death."

"Did he go alone or ask for an attorney?"

"Alone. I think he wanted to be cooperative right now."

"The sheriff may not have evidence against him yet. If they had, they could've arrested him," I told Luke. "But if he said anything self-incriminating, they may use it against him."

"He ... he confessed to making the anonymous nine-one-one call after he saw Kaylee's body."

I gasped. "Was he pressured into confessing?"

"Don't know."

"Did he say anything else besides admitting to making that call?"

"Mike said he kept his mouth pretty much shut after that, seeing how the police had his confession."

"He talked to you about what happened?"

Luke paused, eyeing me as if he wasn't sure what and how much to say to me. "He told me that his car ... he swerved and ran his bumper into a tree. Daniel checked his car over. It was mostly just external damage to the corner of the bumper where it hit the tree. Luckily, it was scrapes and scratches on the car, and Mike wasn't injured."

"I'm glad to hear he's not hurt," I said. "Do you know if Mike swerved before or after he saw Kaylee?"

Luke didn't answer right away.

"What did he tell you?" I asked, softly but firmly.

"I don't remember his exact words. He snapped his fingers and said something like, 'It happened in an instant.'"

"Tell me what you remember."

He swallowed, his Adam's apple moving up. "It was dark. He was driving alone, listening to the radio. He jerked the steering wheel when he saw Kaylee's body on the road and swerved."

"And missed her?"

"Not quite. He didn't miss her completely."

I tried to digest this information. "He didn't miss her completely." Either Mike did or he didn't. If he didn't miss her, then he must have hit her. Luke wasn't being clear.

"Help me out here," I said. "What do you mean by completely?"

He looked down at his shoes.

"He ran over her body? Or a part of it?"

Luke nodded miserably.

It didn't sound good. Mike was at the scene. He saw Kaylee and swerved, but not in time to miss her completely, running over her body.

"Did he..." I couldn't say the word. As if saying it

would make it real. As if saying it would foul the air, and nothing could take it back.

We stared at each other, leaving it unsaid.

CHAPTER TWENTY-FOUR

I was on a mission, driving straight to Mary Belle's house. I had not heard from Betty Lou yet. She had promised to talk to Mary Belle and grease the wheels for my meeting with the grieving mother.

If I let it go for too long, it wouldn't be right. It was a touchy area. To be sympathetic, respectful, and caring. Yet not to be rude or intrusive. But I needed to talk to her about her daughter. And although we didn't make plans for meeting Kaylee's older sister, Sadie, I would like to talk to her too.

By now, the temperature was rising. Another sweltering late-summer day. I rolled up my window and blasted the AC. Time was slipping away. Was Kaylee's death a hit-and-run accident? Luke had added another piece of the puzzle, placing Mike there on the road. Could she have been dead already? If that was the case, did another driver run over her before Mike did? Or could Mike have injured her, and she died then? That did not answer the question of how Kaylee got there, however. Was she already injured and not able to walk or run anymore, so she collapsed on the road?

The questions popped into my mind. The piece about Mike had only added to them. What was he doing there in the middle of the night? Luke didn't have time to give me all the answers. I needed to find out more.

It didn't take long to arrive at Mary Belle's house. I tried my luck again.

An attractive brunette around middle age opened the door when I knocked. The years had added lines to her face. But she was one of the lucky ones who still had a slim figure and aged gracefully.

"Mary Belle." I smiled as I greeted her. "My name is Eve Sawyer. I spoke to Betty Lou the other day."

At the mention of Betty Lou, her face lit up. "Yes, of course. She mentioned you'd come by looking for me. You ... you're that famous journalism student who investigates cases."

I blushed at the compliment, feeling the warmth on my cheeks. "I left my number," I mumbled. "Betty was going to call me."

"Oh, well, I didn't know about that. But I'm glad you're here."

"Perhaps she mentioned that I'd like to have a word with you about Kaylee?"

At the sound of her daughter's name, Mary Belle's shoulders sagged as if the strength that held her up had deflated.

"I'm sorry," I said. This was the part I shied away from. I wished I could relieve some of her pain. I wished I didn't have to bring this up.

Mary Belle collected herself after a while and stepped back. "Please come in."

"Thank you," I said, entering the living room. Framed photos of her and Kaylee and Sadie were displayed on the mantel. A plush oversized sofa looked inviting. But the coffee table exhibited a rebellious indifference, piled with a mess of cluttered drink containers and carelessly tossed mail, food wrappers, and discarded napkins.

Mary Belle waved me to the sofa and took a seat beside me. "So you're the student investigating my Kaylee's accident?"

"Yes. I was traveling through, taking a few days off before school started. When I stopped to eat at Dave's Place, I heard about her." I paused, taking a deep breath. "I saw the roadside memorial. I couldn't get her out of my mind."

"This isn't your first…"

"No, it isn't. But it's a shock every time."

We sat, observing a moment of silence between us.

"I appreciate you meeting with me," I finally said.

"You want to help, right?"

"I want to get to the truth, what happened to Kaylee. The news is casting it as an accident. But the police questioned the man who made the anonymous nine-one-one call."

Mary Belle raised her eyebrow.

"Do you know Mike?" I asked.

"Mike?"

"He's Luke's friend, staying with him at his house."

She nodded. "Is he a suspect?"

"Probably the only person of interest they have with a solid link to the accident. Whether or not it was an accident is still undetermined. I suspect they're doing an autopsy on Kaylee."

"No, not my baby," she suddenly wailed. "They didn't ask me."

"I don't think they have to ask for your permission, Mary Belle. But you can call the coroner's office and check, find out if they need consent from the family."

"What if they've gone ahead with the autopsy?" she asked, her voice shaking.

"I don't know the laws or the process here. The coroner's office should be able to answer your questions and give a status on the determination of the cause and manner of death. I'm sorry I don't know all the answers, but I'd rather not guess and be wrong."

"We don't have a coroner's office here."

"Is it in Bearsville?" I asked.

"Yes, they took her body there. The sheriff's office is also there. I need to make arrangements with the funeral home there too."

"Have you called the funeral home?"

"Yes, but I want to go there and choose the casket

—" Tears welled up in her eyes as she struggled to speak. "But I can't."

I looked around for signs of Sadie, wondering if she knew her mother was so overwhelmed with grief that she hadn't gotten the will or energy to take care of business. "Is Sadie here?"

Mary Belle grunted. "Why?"

"Is she helping you?"

"I haven't seen her since—"

"Mary Belle, I'll take you to Bearsville," I blurted, quickly deciding.

I saw gratitude and relief wash over her face.

"Can we leave in five minutes?" I asked.

She swallowed and slowly nodded.

CHAPTER TWENTY-FIVE

IT WOULD TAKE ABOUT FORTY TO FORTY-FIVE MINUTES to drive to Bearsville, according to the app on my phone. I used my time wisely while waiting in my car for Mary Belle, scoping out the locations for the coroner's and sheriff's offices, and the funeral home, which was a short distance from them.

Although I had spoken in haste when I offered to take Mary Belle there, I realized in hindsight that it was a good plan of action for her, and also for me, seeing as there might be something to uncover about Kaylee's case.

I cranked my engine and turned up the AC, holding my fingers in front of the vents to feel the air flow through. It didn't take long for me to realize Mary Belle and I were not speaking the same language when it came to "five minutes." But I'd give her plenty of slack.

The bright sunlight cheered me up. As did the sight of her approaching my car.

We snapped our seat belts on and went on our way. I snuck a peek at Betty Lou's house as I drove out the driveway. I didn't see her, but the curtain twitched as if someone had jerked back from the window.

The beauty of the countryside was a welcome sight. An expansive land of rolling hills and gentle valleys. Farms and grazing cattle dotted the landscape. Birds flew overhead, making their travels across the crisp blue sky. Wildflowers grew in abundance, mingled with wild grass, bushes, and clumps of rocks.

Mary Belle gazed out the window, perhaps lost in her thoughts. I didn't pry. I had questions about Kaylee that I wanted to bring up, but now was not the time. I relaxed, leaned back, and enjoyed the peaceful drive, taking in the lovely scenery.

CHAPTER TWENTY-SIX

BEARSVILLE WAS THE COUNTY SEAT OF BEAR COUNTY, established in 1834, according to the historical marker.

The county coroner's office was our first stop. It was in a brick building, sharing space with the county sheriff's office. Mary Belle asked me to accompany her, so we went in together.

The assistant, a rail-thin young woman wearing fashionable square-framed glasses, greeted us courteously. After we gave our names and the reason for our visit, she ushered us into a small office with the name-plate "Robert Smith, Coroner" on the door.

"The coroner will be right with you."

"Is he finishing up an autopsy?" I asked.

"No, we have a contracted medical examiner who does autopsies."

"Who orders them?" Mary Belle asked.

"The coroner, when it's his case." The assistant

handed a card to each of us with the coroner's office logo and contact information.

We didn't have to wait long. The coroner came into the office and greeted us warmly, a file folder tucked under his arm. We introduced ourselves and chatted briefly about our trip and the weather. The assistant appeared and offered us bottles of chilled water. We thanked her before she left and closed the door.

"Mrs. Davenport, thank you for coming in to speak to me about your daughter," Robert Smith said, then turned and nodded in my direction. "Ms. Sawyer."

"Thank you for meeting with us," Mary Belle said, doing a good job of holding back signs of anxiety. "I called you yesterday and left a message when you were not available."

"Right, I got your message late in the day. I'm sorry I didn't call you back right away. What can I help you with?"

"Can you tell me how Kaylee died?" Mary Belle Davenport launched right in.

"We are still investigating. Usually, we do the autopsy, gather information, and get the tests done and results back before we make a determination and prepare a final death certificate stating the cause and manner of death."

"How long will that take?"

"It depends. May take weeks to months." He paused. "We just finished her autopsy today," he said. "I wanted to speak with you later, after we were done."

"Was the autopsy necessary?"

He didn't respond right away, as if he was carefully choosing his next words. "Yes. I'm afraid we wouldn't be able to determine her cause of death without it."

She twisted her hands in her lap, shaking her head from side to side, clearly distressed. "You ... you cut up my beautiful child."

He looked uncomfortable, first glancing at her, then at the door that was shut. She stared at him.

Smith raised his hand, displaying the folder he was carrying. He placed it on his desk. "I have the medical examiner's notes."

"Kaylee ..." Mary Belle whispered.

"I'm just going over the notes from the autopsy myself," he said with a cough, keeping his voice gentle and low. "The medical examiner can send out skin, nails, tissue samples, and body fluids for testing, and he will include the results in the final autopsy report."

Mary Belle cocked her head, turning to me. I took it as a cue to jump into the conversation. "Mrs. Davenport is the next of kin. It's important to know what happened to Kaylee and how she died. Can you share the results of the autopsy with her?"

"The written report may take weeks or months to complete. But once it's finished, the next of kin can request a copy of the autopsy report." He nodded in Mary Belle's direction.

I licked my lips. "Is there anything you can say now?" I hoped some information might ease Mary Belle's pain and worry.

The coroner flipped open the folder, glancing at the

few pages of notes. "Hmm..." He frowned, pressing his lips tightly together.

I kept quiet, watching him flip the pages back and forth.

"This is preliminary, and it can't be taken as conclusive."

"Understood," Mary Belle said, leaning forward.

"From the initial examination of the body, it looks like Kaylee had multiple injuries. But..." He paused, giving us a serious look. "But the injuries seem inconsistent."

"Meaning what?" Mary Belle asked, her eyes glued to his lips. "Please explain."

"My impression is that it appears her injuries were not repeats of the same type of injury, and they are in different locations on the body."

Mary Belle had gone completely still, numb with shock.

"Are you able to tell which injury or injuries caused death?" I asked quietly.

"Not at this time. We are investigating, and there's other information from the accident to consider as well."

"Other information?"

"Additional information is being gathered about the case."

"Will you keep me updated?" Mary Belle asked, an insistent and impatient tone in her voice.

"I'll be in touch. If you don't hear from me, please don't hesitate to call."

"Thank you," she said.

As we stood up to leave, I turned back to Smith. "We saw a sign for the sheriff's office coming into the building."

"That's right," he said. "They are on the first floor, down the hall."

"It certainly is convenient," Mary Belle said.

"We will need a signed form from you before we can release Kaylee's body to a funeral home. Have you met with a funeral director?"

"Not yet. I'm going to make arrangements today."

"If you're looking, I think the closest one to your town is the funeral home here. It's one block down the street. We work closely with them to coordinate the release of the body and the transfer to the funeral home."

"I'll meet with them before I leave today."

Smith handed Mary Belle a form. "Please be sure to sign this and bring it back."

CHAPTER TWENTY-SEVEN

Mary Belle and I walked down to the sheriff's office. The receptionist expressed her condolences to the grieving mother when Mary Belle introduced herself and asked to speak to the sheriff. Fortuitously, she could fit us into his schedule now, finding an opening before his next appointment.

I recognized Sheriff Waco immediately from his appearance on television. He was in his uniform, comfortable in his authority and responsibilities. He oozed charm, credibility, and competency, as well as trustworthiness.

Up close, he looked more handsome and burly and tall than I remembered, rising from his desk as we entered his office and gesturing for us to sit in the two chairs facing him. After a round of introductions, we settled in for business.

He addressed Mary Belle first. "Mrs. Davenport, my sympathies."

"Thank you," she said.

"My deputies previously spoke to you about Kaylee." Then he turned to me. "And to you, Ms. Sawyer, about a vandalism incident?"

"Yes, my car was vandalized at Pines Motel and Deputy Clark and Deputy Wilson came to investigate. It may be related to Kaylee's death."

"We've just met with the coroner. I understand you may have new information on Kaylee's case," Mary Belle said, raising her eyebrows in anticipation. "Can you give us an update?"

He nodded. "I talked to the coroner briefly, although I haven't seen the report."

"It was a hit-and-run accident?" she asked.

Waco hesitated before speaking. "It's ... it's actually turning out to be more complicated."

Mary Belle sucked in her breath. "I don't understand," she whispered.

"We're working with the coroner on information from the examination of the body and autopsy, and we're also chasing leads to continue the investigation."

"Can you give us details?" she asked.

"I'm afraid we can't at this time," he said firmly.

Mary Belle and I sat in expectant silence. But no more nuggets of information were forthcoming.

Mary Belle broke the silence with a heavy sigh. "Well, thank you for your time, Sheriff." She turned to me. "Let's go."

I got to my feet, fussing with my purse strap, and followed her out. As I was almost at the door, I suddenly remembered the torn piece of paper I had stuffed in my purse. "Oh, Sheriff?" I pulled out the scrap of paper and showed it to him. "Do you know this number and name?"

He frowned, studying the handwritten scrawl. "What's this?"

I shrugged. "Don't know. Someone left it at the motel."

"What do you want *me* to do with it?" he asked, throwing his hands up.

"Maybe check it out ... out of curiosity."

"Out of curiosity? Hey, I'll do it." He laughed.

I laughed too. "Seriously, can you just write the number down, please?" I watched him do it, then grabbed the piece of paper back. "Thanks, Sheriff."

CHAPTER TWENTY-EIGHT

Mary Belle and I parted ways in front of the building. We arranged to meet back there in thirty minutes, unless we needed more time. She turned left toward the funeral home, and I turned right, remembering a hardware store we had passed coming into Bearsville.

I walked gingerly, avoiding the dogs lying in the shade, and the large bowls of water set out by kind-hearted storekeepers, as some people sought the AC-chilled stores to escape the oppressive heat and humidity.

The hardware store was about two blocks down. I took my time walking there as sweat trickled down my face and chest, sticking to my cotton top. It was a relief when I arrived. Ducking inside, I strolled down the aisles, browsing the neat shelves of products: nuts, bolts, screws, tools, lawn and garden items, cement, wood stains, cans of paint, ropes, buckets, ladders, etc.

"Ma'am, may I help you?" someone said from behind me.

I almost jumped. I was so absorbed that I didn't hear anyone coming up. I whirled around to face a pimply-faced kid. Was this the source of the deep, manly voice?

I grinned. "What did you say?"

"You looking for something?" he asked again.

I pulled out my phone and tapped the photos, finding the one I wanted, a close-up view of the spray paint on my car. "Do you sell spray paint of this color?"

He squinted, bending closer to see. "Ma'am, that's red."

"Yes, but there are different hues. This color is between a bright red and medium red."

"Ma'am, I can't tell real well."

"Have you sold any red spray-paint cans recently?"

"No, ma'am." He scratched his head, then said, "Kyle might have."

I followed the kid as he marched to the register, where an older man with a dour look stood behind it.

"Hey, Kyle, can you help this lady out?" He left me there and disappeared.

I showed Kyle the photo. "Do you have this color of spray paint?"

He stared at the photo. "Aisle C." He led me to the paint aisle, which had a small assortment of spray cans. Kyle took another look at my photo, then picked up a can with a similar color on the label and handed it to me.

I compared the colors, and they were a good match. "Do you remember selling this can?"

"Oh, I sure do," he said, grunting a laugh.

"How are you so sure?" I asked.

"Well, I was busy scanning items for this guy at checkout. When I picked up that can, she thrust out her hand and showed me her nails, which were painted red. Said she liked the color and he'd bought that color in spray paint."

"Wait. A man and woman came in together, and he bought the can after she picked out the color for him?"

"Yep."

"What did the guy look like?"

"Oh, I'd say he was older, in his forties, thin."

"And the woman?"

"It was the girl on TV."

A sinking feeling of dread filled my stomach. "The girl?" I stuttered.

"Yeah, the dead girl in the hit-and-run."

CHAPTER TWENTY-NINE

I ARRIVED A FEW MINUTES EARLY AT THE COUNTY OFFICE building. Mary Belle appeared right on time.

"Be right back," she said, waving the signed release form as she popped inside.

I waited outside, resting under the portico shading the front entrance. Absorbed in thought, going over the events of the day, I didn't hear Mary Belle approach. She tapped my shoulder to get my attention. "All done."

My throat was dry and my feet ached, but I was not ready to head back to the motel yet. "What do you want to do next?"

"How about a tall glass of sweet iced tea and a bite to eat?"

"Sounds great," I said, smiling.

"It's my treat." Mary Belle flashed a relaxed smile. "I've been wanting to go to Sweet Peas. It's just a short walk from here."

Sweet Peas was a charming little restaurant. Inside, the walls were painted a pastel green, with drawings of twirling vines, leaves, and sweet peas nestled in pods.

It was late afternoon and not crowded yet, allowing us to be quickly seated at a table in a quiet corner. The waitress took our orders and then brought us our iced teas.

My bowl of sweet pea soup came quickly after, followed by a grilled cheese sandwich. Mary Belle had the daily special, country fried steak and gravy with mashed potatoes and turnip greens.

The food was delicious, the iced tea just right, not saccharine sweet. We engaged in light conversation as we concentrated on eating.

We got refills of our iced tea as the waitress cleared our plates.

I was content, my hunger satisfied.

"How was it?" Mary Belle asked.

"That was a mighty tasty meal. Thank you, Mary Belle."

"No need. I'm the one who needs to thank you," she said, picking at her crumpled napkin. "I wanted to be left alone ... didn't have the strength ... couldn't go out. But I needed forcing to get out of the house and get these things done. You drove me here and took me to the coroner's and sheriff's offices. And I got to pick out a casket and put down a deposit."

"I know it's hard. You feel like you're alone. But you're not alone now. We did this together."

She nodded, eyes misting.

"Tell me about Kaylee, if you feel like talking," I said.

Mary Belle sighed. "I loved her so much. But I didn't say it often enough. I was raised that way. I thought she'd know even when I didn't say it. Kaylee was my pride and joy. When she was a baby—" She wiped her tear-stained face with the back of her hand as her lips quivered. "What am I going to do without her?"

"The sheriff said it's turning out to be more complicated," I said, gently guiding the conversation. "What if ... what if it wasn't just a hit-and-run?"

Mary Belle stared at me with a blank look on her face. "You mean ..."

"Can you think of anyone who'd want to kill her?"

"Nobody," she said, shaking her head. "Not my Kaylee."

"When was the last time you saw her that day?" I asked.

"Well ..." She rubbed her forehead. "Kaylee had the evening shift, from four to ten. I dropped her off at work and then came home."

"Did you see her after work?"

"She mentioned meeting someone after work, and she'd get a ride home. Told me not to wait up. So I went to bed early."

"Did she say who?"

"I assumed it was one of her friends."

"Was that unusual?"

Mary Belle thought a bit. "No, she didn't always come straight back home after work."

"I went to the hardware store, and someone there said Kaylee was with a guy who bought a can of spray paint there. Know anything about it?"

"No, but she likes to come here to shop for clothes and things. People drive here to get stuff we can't get back home in Vain. There's always somebody who'll give her a ride." She paused. "Was he sure it was Kaylee?"

"The guy recognized her from TV—you know, from her picture."

Mary Belle gave a slight head shake, looking tired.

We drove home after we had eaten. Mary Belle fell asleep in the car on the way back.

After I dropped her off, I drove straight to my motel. I was also exhausted, but I needed to do one more thing before I went to bed. I called the number written on the paper I found in my room and left a message asking Jimmy to call me back. I fell asleep soon after I hung up.

CHAPTER THIRTY

The next morning, I woke up to the sound of my ringing phone. I was groggy when I answered.

"Hi, Eve?" a man's voice asked.

"Uh, who's this?" I stammered.

"Lance Spencer. Remember me?"

It was coming back to me. At the roadside memorial. "Oh yes."

"Hey, how's the investigation going?"

I yawned, clearly not in a frame of mind to discuss this yet.

"I heard you've been having a rough spell," he said. "Thought you might want some cheering up."

"I can handle it," I said. "Thanks, but no thanks."

"How would you like to go fishing?"

I rubbed my eyes, seeing the time on the bedside clock. I'd overslept. Going fishing was the last thing on my mind.

"How about it?"

"Can I take a rain check?" I said. "I don't know how to fish."

"I know you've been asking about Kaylee. I'd like to talk to you more about her. How about a drive, then? C'mon, I'll take you to Kaylee's favorite fishing spot."

At the mention of Kaylee's name, I couldn't refuse. Maybe I could find out more about her. Some useful information. I was stumped, and maybe this could help. I got off the bed and headed toward the bathroom. "Okay, give me some time. I need coffee and breakfast first. Meet you in an hour?"

"I'll swing by and pick you up," he said.

"You know where I'm at?"

He laughed. "Pines Motel. It's the only motel here."

LANCE WAS right on time pulling into the parking lot. I was waiting outside.

I climbed into the truck, grabbing the door handrail to pull up to the seat.

"Ready?" he asked.

"Yep," I said as I snapped the seat belt in.

It was smooth going on the asphalt before Lance turned onto a dirt road partially filled with gravel. It was bumpy, and something under my seat rolled, resting against my feet. I kicked it back, and it rolled forward again at the next curve of the road, irritating me continuously until we stopped when we reached the fishing spot.

Lance parked on a small embankment overlooking the water. A narrow trail led down to the water's edge. "We're here," he said, opening his door.

I opened my door and leaned down to see what was rolling under my seat. That's when I saw it—the can of spray paint. Though part of the label was hidden, I recognized it. The same one I'd seen in the hardware store. The same one Kyle had said was purchased by the man Kaylee was with.

"You coming?" Lance yelled as he climbed out of the driver's seat, getting ready to close his door.

I looked up, straightening my back. Our eyes locked.

He saw. He knew. In an instant, he moved like a flash of lightning, rushing around his truck toward me.

I grabbed the can, jumped out, and ran. I tried to get as far and fast as I could away from him. But I was no match for him. I stumbled over loose pebbles and fell, then got up and ran some more. Lance chased me down and grabbed me, his fingers squeezing my arms, nails digging into my skin as I teared up in pain. I dropped the can.

The rage on his face was terrifying, transforming him into a grotesque fiend. I squeezed my eyes shut, trembling with fear. He shook me like a rag doll and threw me down, kicking me while I was on the ground. I screamed as he approached for a second round. I rolled over and scrambled sideways. He came at me. I fought back, reaching out to grab anything I could use

—a rock, a stick—and came up with a fistful of dirt. I flung it at his face, but my aim was off and it fell short.

He laughed, cracking his knuckles.

My fingers probed the ground, pawing the soil, searching for a weapon. My brain was trying to comprehend what was happening. What it meant. Tying it together. The red spray-paint can. A surge of adrenaline rushed through my body as my fingers touched the can. Grasped it. I held it with both hands, aimed the nozzle at Lance's face, and pressed it, shooting for his eyes.

He was yelling, flailing wildly, and desperately trying to get the paint out of his eyes. As Lance stumbled and hesitated, not knowing which way to turn, I took off, running to his truck.

The key was still in the ignition. I started the engine and stepped on the gas, reaching in my purse for my phone and dialing the sheriff.

CHAPTER THIRTY-ONE

He answered on the first ring.

"Sheriff Waco," I said, shouting between brief gasps of breath.

"Hold on, is this Eve?"

"Yes," I panted, steering the truck on the bumpy road.

"Well, I was just going to call you—"

"Help!" I screamed, interrupting him.

"Eve, what happened?"

"He ... he attacked me," I said, my voice shaking.

"Eve, where are you?" he shouted.

"I'm driving his truck," I sputtered, my pulse racing. "Lance ... left him back by the fishing spot."

"Wait—Lance who?"

"Lance Spencer. He ... he's after me!" I screamed.

"He's after you?"

"Yes, he's the attacker," I yelled. "Please hurry."

"Hold on," he said.

I couldn't make out the faint conversation. The sheriff came back on the line. "Deputy Clark and Deputy Wilson are in the area. Clark knows where the fishing spot is. They know who Lance is. They're heading your way."

I let out a sigh, then remembered what he said about calling me. "What was it you wanted to tell me?"

"The paper with the phone number."

"You have Jimmy's last name for me?" I pressed the phone tight against my ears.

"Anderson."

I repeated his full name. "Jimmy Anderson."

"That's right."

"Thanks, Sheriff."

LANCE WAS ARRESTED and transported to the Bearsville Hospital, where he would get treatment for his eye injury first. I was asked if I wanted treatment, but I declined, preferring ice, a wrap, and some rest.

It was nice to be settled in bed with everything within easy reach. I arranged my phone, notebook, and pen closest to me. I still felt traumatized about what happened with Lance. Why didn't he want me around? Why was he trying to scare me away? Did he have something to hide?

I must have dozed off because the next thing I knew, the shrill ringing from my cell phone woke me up. I was on top of the bedcovers, fully dressed except for my shoes.

"Hello?" I said.

"I got your message," a man's voice said.

"What ... who is this?"

"Jimmy," he said. "You the lady who has my stuff?"

I turned up the volume on my cell. My heartbeat raced in my chest. I had left a brief voicemail that I found something of his. It was true. The piece of paper with his first name and phone number. I just didn't go into detail.

"That's me," I replied cheerfully, trying to tone down my excitement. "Eve Sawyer."

"Where can I pick it up?"

I had to think fast. If I mentioned the motel, he might figure out why I was calling. But I didn't want to spook him before I had a chance to ask him some questions.

"How about we meet? Is Bearsville close to you?"

Jimmy paused. Silence stretched between us, and I worried that he'd hang up. Finally, I heard a sigh. "I can meet you there in two hours."

"Do you know Sweet Pea?"

"Yeah, meet you there."

CHAPTER THIRTY-TWO

I picked the same table at Sweet Pea where I'd sat before, arriving early, ten minutes before our scheduled meeting time. I'd given myself plenty of time to get ready and drive, being careful not to exert myself. I'd described to Jimmy what I looked like and would wear, and he did the same.

I nursed my iced tea as I sat facing the entrance.

Jimmy was right on time. He stood in the doorway, looking around for me. I raised my hand and waved, catching his attention, motioning him over to the table.

I watched the stocky man in his forties as he maneuvered between the tables gracefully. He had a full head of dark hair tied in a ponytail and a trimmed beard tinged with gray.

"Eve Sawyer?" he said.

I recognized his deep voice immediately. "Jimmy."

"Anderson," he finished.

We shook hands and took our seats.

The waitress glided to our table and got his drink order, bringing back another tall glass of iced tea for Jimmy.

He sipped his drink and waited.

I cleared my throat. "Thank you for coming."

He gave a hesitant nod.

"I hope it wasn't out of your way," I said. "I wasn't sure if you'd come."

"I'm here," he said. "You have something for me?"

I reached into my purse and took out the piece of paper, sliding it across the table. "Is this your hand-writing?"

His cheeks reddened. He sat still, not touching it. "Where did you get this?"

"At the Pines Motel."

Jimmy didn't move, his eyes fixed on the paper.

"Room number six," I said.

He jerked his head up, giving me an incredulous stare. "How did you find this?"

"It was caught up in the lamp cord behind the nightstand. Is this yours?"

He answered with a slight nod and a sigh.

"I'm in that room now," I said. "When were you there?"

"A few days ago. But I didn't really check out."

"So it *was* you," I said. "The motel staff thought you had left. You were supposed to have checked out. You hadn't booked another night. They gave me the room."

"I paid cash for my room." He glanced around nervously. "I used a fake name when I checked in."

"And a fake number?" I asked, assuming it was bogus also.

"Yeah," he muttered.

"But you left your stuff in the room?"

"I couldn't go back. I had intended to check out." His eyebrows furrowed. "So what happened to my things?"

"I think they put it in storage. Don't know for how long. If you don't go back, they'll probably get rid of it."

He raked his fingers through his hair. "Thank you for contacting me."

"Look, it's not my business," I said. "But why didn't you go back?"

Jimmy had kept his eyes downcast. When he looked up, I saw the sadness in his eyes—so deep, it was like he was drowning in it. Like he was a broken man, and his world had fallen apart. Like he was a lost soul.

"I'm sorry." I touched his arm softly. "Do you want to talk about it?"

CHAPTER THIRTY-THREE

Once Jimmy Anderson started talking, it was like a valve had opened, releasing a flood of words. He spoke slowly at first, then they tumbled out. I sat and listened intently, at times interrupting him before he finished.

This was his story:

"I was the no-tipper at the diner. I had tracked Kaylee down and knew she worked at Dave's Place," Jimmy said.

"Why didn't you tip?" I asked.

"It was my first time meeting Kaylee since she was a baby."

"Wait—you knew her as a baby?"

He averted his eyes, looking down at the table. "I am her father."

"You're Kaylee Davenport's father?" I frowned.

"Yes."

"Um, but you're Jimmy Anderson. Did you change your last name?"

"No, Mary Belle reverted back to her maiden name and changed Kaylee's name after our divorce."

I processed that information and let it sink in. "And you had agreed to Kaylee's surname change?" I murmured.

"That's right." He spread his hands, palms up, like he was starting to pray. "I don't have any excuses. I was no good as a husband or father. I ran away from my responsibilities. I drifted from job to job and place to place. Got into trouble. I loathed every bit of myself. It went from bad to worse. I thought I couldn't fall any lower. But I did."

There was no sign of the former man sitting in front of me. The Jimmy who was speaking now was well-dressed and well-groomed. He looked healthy. He was polite and had an air of self-confidence. "What happened to your old self?"

He grunted. "That's a long story. Maybe for another time. Suffice to say that my life changed after I fell asleep on a church pew one night and woke up to a second chance."

"So back to the diner," I prodded with a smile.

"I was nervous and didn't sleep well the night before," Jimmy said, running his fingers through his hair. "My anxiety level was so through the roof that I forgot to bring my wallet. Can you imagine my horror when I reached for my wallet, and it wasn't there? I couldn't pay for my meal, let alone the tip."

"So she—"

"She covered my meal when I told her what

happened. She told me not to worry about it. And that things happen."

"Did Kaylee know you were her father then?"

"Not yet. I hadn't told her. Kaylee was kind to a stranger."

"You palmed her the note then?"

"Yes." He picked up the torn paper with his name and number. "I vowed to myself I'd come back and make amends."

"Did you go back to the diner multiple times?"

"Yes, although sometimes I didn't see Kaylee, and it was another waitress."

"But you spent some time with Kaylee?"

"We talked. I told her bits of my history. Asked her about her life and aspirations." His eyes prickled with tears.

"Tell me about the last time you saw her," I said softly.

Jimmy's eyes went distant. "We had planned to meet after her evening shift ended. She had decided to leave town, and I wanted to give her a surprise before she left. I had finally told her I was her father." He gave a sad smile. "It was supposed to be a celebration."

"So you rented a room at the motel?" I asked.

"Yes, that one time. Previously, I'd go and eat at the diner, and then leave without staying overnight."

"What time did you see Kaylee?"

"It was shortly after ten thirty when she knocked on the door. I opened it. We hugged, and then she came in, clutching the note I'd written." Jimmy paused, wrinkling his brow in a scowl.

"So that's how the note ended up back at the motel room," I mused. "Then what?"

"I glimpsed movement in the dark, and a man appeared after her. I heard Kaylee call out his name in surprise—Lance—as he charged into the room. He grabbed Kaylee from behind and pinned her to him with his arm hooked around her neck, in a chokehold, using his other hand to pull her head back, exposing her throat. He backed up to the door. I yelled, 'Don't hurt her.' I charged, rushing forward to attack him. Lance warned me not to come any closer. As soon as he focused on me, Kaylee struggled, grabbed his arm, and dug in with her nails. She fought and stomped hard on his foot. He recoiled and lost his grip."

I was hanging on Jimmy's every word. "What happened next?"

"Kaylee was free, away from Lance. I yelled at her to get behind me. Lance rushed me in a tackle, slamming me against the wall, punched me in the stomach and kneed me in the groin. I doubled over. Lance punched me hard on the jaw. I stumbled, dazed. The last thing I heard was Kaylee yelling at him to stop, and that he was killing me. Then Lance hit me again, and I blacked out."

CHAPTER THIRTY-FOUR

I CALLED SHERIFF WACO AND BROUGHT HIM UP TO speed. The sheriff's office was our next stop. Jimmy was going there to tell his story—what he had just told me. There was only one person, Lance, who could tell us what happened after Jimmy had blacked out.

By the time we entered the building, I had gotten a call back from Waco. Lance was still at the hospital, where he'd been waiting to be seen by a doctor. The ER had had its hands full with a fire. If I wanted to talk to him now, I'd have to get over there pronto. The sheriff said he'd talked to Deputy Wilson, who was there with Deputy Clark. They would allow me a few minutes to visit Lance if he agreed. Of course, he would be under guard and handcuffed to the bed.

I quickly said goodbye to Jimmy. I lost no time driving to the hospital, which was not far.

I GRABBED a chair and pulled it next to the hospital bed. The deputy on guard was nearby and visible. I sat facing Lance. I knew now that Lance was capable of violence, but extreme violence? Murder? Could Lance be Kaylee's killer?

I cleared my throat, then waited for him to turn his paint-streaked, smeared face toward me. "How's your eye?" I asked.

He squinted at me with his left eye. A patch covered his right one. He faced away from me to look at the ceiling.

"Did they wash out your eyes and put on the patch?"

I watched his reaction. A slight nod.

"They're treating people from a fire incident," I said calmly and quietly. "The doctor should be with you soon." I put my face inches from the guardrail. "Lance, I only have a few minutes. Will you talk to me?"

No answer.

I wondered why he was reluctant to speak. Was he afraid someone would overhear? "Look, how about this? I ask you some questions, and you answer with a nod."

Here goes, I thought to myself.

"That last night, did you follow Kaylee to the motel after her shift ended?"

I watched for his reaction—no answer.

"Did you follow Kaylee into the room?"

No answer.

"You saw the man she was meeting?"

No answer.

"Know who he was?"

No answer.

"Know why she was meeting him?"

No answer.

"Did you know the real reason—that he's her father?"

He whipped his head, turning to face me.

"So that's why you were so mad?" I asked.

He bared his teeth, sneering. "That no-good, scumbag piece of shit left her when she was a baby!" he spat out, spittle flying. "I was her father. I raised her. I took care of her."

"She was his baby," I said.

"So now he comes slinking back into her life and"—he threw out a sharp laugh—"and ... and she's thrown me aside like I'm nothing?"

"You wanted to kill him? And her?"

No answer.

"You thought he was dead back in the room?"

I detected a slight nod.

"You went after Kaylee, maybe choked her again? You killed her?"

No answer.

"Why'd you leave Kaylee?"

No answer.

"You panicked and fled, didn't you?"

No answer.

I laid it on thick, shouting in his face, "Thought you'd killed her too. And you ran away like a coward!"

The look on his face said it all—the guilt. The remorse. The sorrow.

CHAPTER THIRTY-FIVE

LANCE COULD NOT CONTROL HIS RAGE. JIMMY HAD faced it. Kaylee had too. But unbeknownst to Lance, Jimmy had not died.

We left Bearsville late in the afternoon.

Jimmy came back to the motel and retrieved his things after paying the storage fee. I asked him why he left them, and Jimmy said after he woke up in his room, alone, he'd looked for Kaylee and didn't find her. Kaylee was gone, and he was afraid Lance would come back and finish him off. Jimmy left in a hurry and fled from the motel without looking back, not taking the time to pack. It wasn't until later that he heard on the news that Kaylee was dead. I asked Jimmy if he'd come forward and told anyone. He shamefully confessed that he'd run away and told no one. He wondered if anyone would believe him, given his background. He'd be a suspect.

The sheriff's deputies were taking over Room 6,

securing it as a crime scene. They were unsuccessful in getting video footage from the motel security camera.

The motel offered me a free night's stay in another room. I packed up my stuff and moved.

I thought about Lance. I tossed and turned all night, replaying the scene Jimmy had described over and over. It had happened two doors down. I shivered, wrapping the covers around my body like a cocoon. I squeezed my eyes shut, unable to sleep.

Was it all over? I should feel relieved. I should sleep like a baby.

Throughout the restless night, sleep escaped me.

CHAPTER THIRTY-SIX

I woke up on a bright morning. It was another beautiful summer day. The sky was clear and blue.

I still had a bit of time to enjoy the last days of summer before school started. But first, before I left here, I needed to pay another visit to Kaylee's mom.

Betty Lou called me as I was driving there.

"Eve," she said, "you still want to meet with Sadie?"

I had almost forgotten about Sadie. "Oh course! I missed her on my last visit."

"Well, dearie, you're in luck. Sadie came home last night. It was late, and I didn't want to bother you then."

"No, this is good. I'm glad you called." I still wanted to ask Sadie some questions.

"Between her mother and me, we've brought Sadie up to speed."

THEY WERE WAITING for me when I arrived at Mary Belle's house.

Betty Lou had brought over her cinnamon buns, and Mary Belle had brewed a fresh pot of coffee. We sat down in the living room. Sadie came out of the kitchen carrying three mugs of steaming coffee and then three small plates. She set them down next to the tray of buns.

Mary Belle introduced me. "Sadie, this is Eve Sawyer. She's been working on Kaylee's case and was a big help to me." Sadie was a fresh-faced, plain-looking girl. I couldn't really see a resemblance between her and her younger half sister.

"Pleased to meet you," she said.

"Likewise." I smiled. "I was hoping to see you. Were you away?"

Her cheeks reddened. Sadie looked down at her bun and dropped it back on her plate. "It's complicated."

"Are you still conflicted?" I asked.

She raised her head and looked straight at me. "Not anymore."

"Why don't you start by telling me where you were?"

Sadie looked at her mother and Betty Lou before turning her gaze back to me. "I was with Danielle."

Betty Lou cried out in surprise, her mouth falling open. "You were with my daughter?"

"I made her promise not to say anything to you, so don't blame her."

"But why?"

Sadie drew a deep breath. "I couldn't deal with it. Kaylee's death, Mom, everything. I had to get away, and the only person I knew in the city was Danielle."

"I didn't know you kept up with her," Betty Lou whispered.

"We've stayed in touch. We talked, and Danielle invited me to stay with her. I left a note with Mom that I was at a friend's and not to worry about me."

"We're just glad you're back and safe," Mary Belle said. "But promise me you won't disappear like that again without talking to me."

"I can't promise that. We'll have to work on our relationship first, Mom."

Mary Belle looked embarrassed and blushed.

"Well, tell us why you're back," Betty Lou said.

"Danielle told me you'd called and said Mom was having a hard time. I was selfish in leaving." She swallowed a sip of coffee. "Mom needed me, and I wasn't here."

"Hon, you're back now and that's what matters," Mary Belle said, holding Sadie's hand and giving a gentle pat.

"Do you remember anything about your sister that last day?" I asked.

"I saw Kaylee in the morning before her shift. She was laying out some stuff to take with her, and I had asked what she was doing."

"What did she say?"

"She showed me. It was a black lace-trimmed top and white pants and new sandals in the box."

"Did she say what the occasion was?"

Sadie smiled. "She said it was a celebration. I tried to weasel more information out of her, but she wouldn't tell me. We were laughing and joking. I teased her. Finally, to put a stop to me, she put on the outfit and shoes and told me to take a picture of her."

"Show me the photo."

Sadie pulled out her phone and the photo of Kaylee —smiling, glowing with excitement in her fetching outfit and sandals. "There," she said, holding it up for all of us to see.

"Can you zoom in?" I asked.

Sadie made the adjustment, and I took the phone. I viewed the photo slowly from top to bottom, stopping when I reached Kaylee's feet. I stared. My hands trembled.

"What is it?" Sadie asked, her voice shaky.

"She was wearing her new sandals?"

"Yeah."

I zoomed in closer. A sudden cold seized my chest. I shook my head.

"What's wrong?" Sadie leaned in, peering over my shoulder.

"I've seen this flower," I croaked. "The rhinestone flowers on her shoes! We've got to contact the sheriff and send him this photo."

I pulled out my phone and dialed Sheriff Waco.

THE SHERIFF's office got a warrant and searched Luke's house. They found the rhinestone flower in the crevice between the sofa cushions, where I had found it and tucked it back in place. They had Kaylee's sandals from the scene, and one shoe was missing the rhinestone flower, which must have come loose and fallen off in Luke's car. He had stuffed it in his pants pocket and went home, where it later fell out onto the sofa, in between the cushions.

CHAPTER THIRTY-SEVEN

There was one more person I wanted to talk to.

I drove to Luke's house. I turned into the driveway and parked. A car was there with the driver's door open, and what appeared to be someone sitting inside. I got out and walked slowly, taking measured steps toward the vehicle.

The man had his eyes closed, head thrown back on the headrest.

"Mike," I said softly, recognizing him.

He didn't answer or move.

I broke out in a cold sweat. Was he okay? I eased closer and watched the gentle rise and fall of his breathing. It was then that I saw the crushed aluminum beer cans strewn on the passenger seat and the floor of the car.

What was he doing? Was he drunk? Sleeping it off?

"Mike," I said, keeping my voice low and even. "Wake up." I leaned closer until my lips were inches from his ear. "Mike!" I barked, shaking his arm with a gentle touch.

His eyelids flickered open, staring blankly until his gaze focused on me. Mike shifted his body, turning away, and settled into a more relaxed position by resting his head in the crook of his arm.

I reacted quickly, and without thinking, honking the car horn.

He jumped at the loud blast and scrambled to sit up, yelling and cursing like a sailor.

IT TOOK some time before Mike could talk to me. He went into the house to clean up. When he emerged from the bathroom, he had on a fresh T-shirt and jeans. His hair was still damp from the shower.

"How are you feeling?" I asked.

"Like I have a splitting headache."

"Do you have any aspirin?"

He shrugged.

"How about I make a pot of coffee?" I asked. "Don't know how much it'll help, but it can't hurt."

He smiled weakly. "Okay."

I went into the kitchen and found the coffeemaker. I hustled quickly to get the coffee brewing. When it was ready, I grabbed two clean mugs, poured coffee, and joined Mike in the living room.

I sipped my coffee, watching Mike do the same. "Feeling better?" I asked after a few minutes.

"Yes, thanks."

"Any word about Luke?"

"The sheriff's department detained Luke and questioned him. He's still in custody."

"They searched this place?"

"Yes."

"After Luke and Kaylee broke up, was Luke still keeping in touch with her?"

"Luke and Kaylee had set up location sharing on their phones and hadn't turned it off."

"Did Luke tell you about the night Kaylee died?"

Mike let out a huge breath and nodded. "Yeah, he told me."

I waited.

"Luke said he had tried to meet up with her after work. After not being able to reach her, he used the phone app to track Kaylee's location to the motel. He found her there, she was hurt, and he carried her out to his car, intending to take her to the hospital."

"Did he see anyone else in the room?"

"Yeah, he mentioned seeing a man passed out on the floor and he left him there as he rushed to his car with Kaylee in his arms."

"He didn't see anyone else?" I asked, thinking of Lance fleeing the scene. Where was he?

"No."

"So Kaylee was still alive?"

"Yeah, I asked him. But Luke said she wasn't responsive. He couldn't wake her up. He grabbed Kaylee and shook her to ask her about the man back at the motel. He wanted to know who he was, why she was meeting him there, and the unthinkable—had she gone to the motel to have sex with this man?"

"Did he give her CPR or something?"

Mike shook his head. "He didn't say. It didn't help that Luke had been drinking and fuming for hours when Kaylee didn't call him back. That man with Kaylee ... that was the straw that broke the camel's back. Luke was consumed with jealousy. Enraged and driven mad, he ...."

He paused, taking time to regain control. "When he realized he'd killed her, he drove back on the highway and dumped her on the road."

"But you made the nine-one-one call?" I frowned.

Mike lowered his head. "Yes, I'd run over someone on the road as I was driving here to stay at Luke's house." His voice cracked. "I ... I didn't know it was Kaylee."

"Where did you make the phone call?"

"I stopped at an old gas station near here. It was closed, but they had a pay phone outside."

I sighed, thinking how sad this was, how things didn't work out for Kaylee, how her life was cut short before she could realize her dreams. The tragedy of it all. "When did Luke tell you this?"

"Yesterday."

I squeezed his hand, finally understanding what had happened, why Mike was drunk in his car.

CHAPTER THIRTY-EIGHT

I left Vain the next day.

I drove back home to spend the last day of my summer vacation with Mom before heading back to campus. I couldn't wait to see her—and tell her how much I loved her.

EPILOGUE

Authorities charged Luke Adams with murder in the death of Kaylee Davenport. Luke had dumped her body on the highway to make it look like a hit-and-run. The autopsy confirmed that she was dead before a vehicle ran her over. The medical examiner ruled Kaylee Davenport's death a homicide.

Mike was not charged. The security camera footage from the gas station near Luke's house captured his image where he made the 911 call. The investigation showed that another driver had also run over Kaylee as well. However, the unknown driver did not call 911.

Lance Spencer faced additional charges in relation to his assaults on Kaylee Davenport and Jimmy Anderson.

Mary Belle Davenport and Jimmy reconnected at Kaylee's funeral. They found support in each other in their shared grief.

Jimmy Anderson visited Kaylee's grave often. He'd

looked back with regret at what he'd done—riddled with guilt for abandoning his child and his failure to protect his daughter at the end. The anonymous note, "I will miss you like no other," was written by him. Kaylee's death ignited his quest for redemption. He remained faithful and committed to doing good works for the rest of his life.

ABOUT THE AUTHOR

Jane Suen is an award-winning author who writes mysteries, sci-fi thrillers, short stories, contemporary romance, and crime fiction.

While driving through Alabama on a hot summer afternoon, she saw a "Murder Creek" road sign which inspired her first book in the Eve Sawyer Mystery series. *Death in Vain* is her sixth book in the series.

Primal Will

SHORT STORIES

Beginnings and Endings: A Selection of Short Stories

I Ain't Afraid of Nothin'